ENIGMA SQUAD

The Case of the
Bike in the Birdcage

Brian C. Jacobs

*Hudson -
Never stop Reading!
Free Your imagination!*

www.EnigmaSquad.com

Excite Kids Press
Seattle, WA

www.EnigmaSquad.com

Published 2012
First Excite Kids Press trade paperback printing
November 2011

15 14 13 12 11   1 2 3 4 5

Library of Congress Control Number: 2011942984

ISBN 978-1-936672-19-6

Printed in Grand Rapids, MI, U.S.A.

Distributed to the trade by Seattle Book Company
seattlebookcompany.com

For my dear Annabelle,

Thank you for continuing to show me how

to think outside the box.

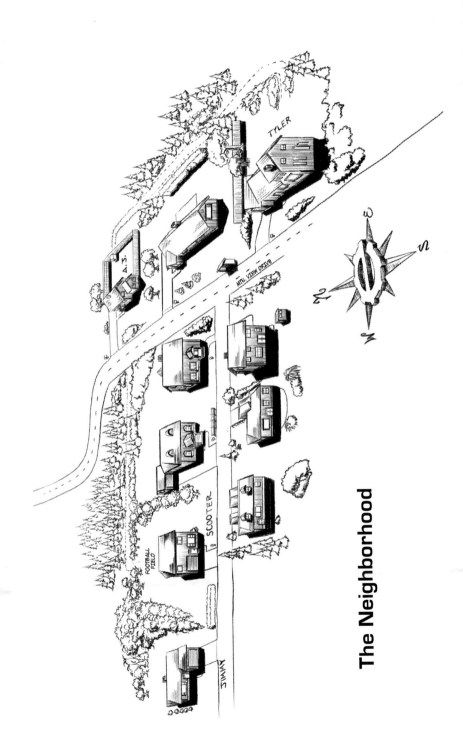

The Neighborhood

The Case of the
Bike in the Birdcage

Brian C. Jacobs

CHAPTER 1
Burger, Fries, and a Surprise

Okay. Maybe we got in over our heads a little this time. After previously stopping an international crime spree, I'd have thought this case would be a piece of cake—boy, was I wrong! In fact, if it weren't for a little help from an unlikely source, I might still be cleaning dirt out of my ears! Unlike last time, I'm not documenting this for the police. They are all-too-familiar with this case as it is. No, this case file is for internal use only! I'm just trying to record all the relevant facts so we can discuss them at some later date, because honestly, after this case, I'm not even sure I know who's pulling the strings anymore...

This is Tyler Pate, Chief Recordkeeping Officer for the Enigma Squad. That's not an official title or anything, but since Scooter and AJ make me do all the recordkeeping, I can give myself whatever title I want! If you read about our first case, *The Case of the Old Man in the Mailbox*, then you know that AJ, Scooter, and I have started our very own detective agency and called it the Enigma Squad. If you haven't read the previous case file, well, then you should. (It's pretty good if I do say so myself!) But just in case you haven't read it, let me fill you in on some details I might otherwise forget to mention as I document this next whirlwind of a case.

First of all, the three of us live in the Westridge neighborhood in the quiet town of Silverdale, Washington. As a detective agency, we're still young, only a couple months old, but we're pretty good.

The Enigma Squad has three members: Scooter, AJ, and me. Scooter Parks ("Sean," to his mom and *no one* else!) is the brains of our organization. He's a mechanical wizard, always tinkering with something—a robotic blender, motion-sensing lightbulbs, or a mechanical dog-walker (AJ's dog didn't like being the guinea pig for that one!). Scooter can usually find an answer to a question before the rest of us know that there *is* a question.

AJ Seeva is the muscle of the group. He's pretty popular in school, good-looking (if you can believe what girls say), and athletic. He plays just about every sport there is, but his grades are... well, let's just say they aren't as good as Scooter's. That might be putting it too nicely. That's kind of like saying asparagus doesn't taste as good as Mint Chocolate Chip ice cream—duh! Anyway, AJ is strong and fast, and he's a really good friend.

I guess I'm the mouth. I might be Mr. Average at just about everything—grades, sports, height, you

3-1 5-20 10-8 6-4 15-3 8-12 5-11 24-4 29 6-6 16-15 1-13

name it—but I'm pretty good at talking. I think it's a survival skill, something I developed so that AJ and Scooter (two guys who are very cool in very different ways) will keep hanging out with a dork like me. It comes in handy, though: Scooter usually takes too long to say just the right thing, and AJ usually doesn't hesitate to say just the wrong thing. So I've figured out how to quickly say something that will at least get us out of trouble. Well, now you should have enough to proceed with this case file.

So this case began a couple weeks after school was out for the summer. Scooter, AJ and I decided to kick off our summer with a short hiking trip to Lower Lena Lake in the Olympic Mountains. We love to hike during the summer months, especially up in the Olympics. There are some very grueling hikes out there with some pretty cool stuff to see. This hike was different, though. Lower Lena is an easy hike; in fact, it's so easy that a lady from church completed the whole thing while she was eight months pregnant!

Anyway, we decided to do an easy hike this time around because AJ's dad was the only parent available to take us, and he was only available for a short overnight hike squished in between Friday and Saturday afternoons. My dad was the real backpacker out of all the parents, and he was stuck out at sea with the Navy until later in the summer. When he got back, we would go on a *real* hike to someplace like Mt. Ellinor or Staircase. Yes, a hike with

8-3 10-14 24-3 3-8 5-20 6-4 2-1 16-16 5-3 6-3 10-6 5-23

a name like Staircase *is* as grueling as it sounds. Plus, my dad would make sure we had time for a real hike. You gotta stay out in the wild for a couple days before you can claim you were really roughing it. Anything less than that, and you are just loaning your body to the mosquitoes for nothing! The other way to know you're roughing it is when you have to "clean" your water before you can drink it. There is nothing like dying of thirst while having to boil water and then get it to cool down enough to drink. But like I said, this trip was not one of those. This was a quick weekend trip to enjoy the great outdoors, knowing the next day of school was a good two months away.

As is our custom whenever we take a trip to the Olympic Mountains, on our way home we stopped by our favorite burger place in the whole universe: Fat Smitty's. I knew I would like Fat Smitty's even before I stepped inside the first time. Outside the front door, you see this huge, six-foot-tall wooden burger that was carved by a chainsaw.

But once you get inside, you see where the real beauty of Fat Smitty's is. There are dollar bills and business cards tacked to every inch of wall space in the entire restaurant. For probably two decades, people have been writing messages on dollars and then tacking them to the walls wherever they could find space. The ceiling is also crowded with dollar bills, each tacked on one end, with the rest of the bill hanging down so that it looks like grass is growing from the ceiling. Whenever the door opens—and it opens *a lot*—the bells attached to the door handle clang, and the rush of air makes the whole ceiling do the wave as paper bills flap around.

The first time I was at Fat Smitty's, I spent so much time staring at the ceiling and reading messages on the walls that I almost forgot about the food. But forgetting about the food is really hard to do! The Fat Smitty burger is their specialty and is the biggest burger I have ever laid eyes on. I am not kidding: it is almost as big as my head. We boys always get a laugh because we have to stand up and put all our weight on top of the burgers to squish them down small enough just to be able to fit them in our mouths!

And if the burgers were not enough, the milkshakes might even be better. Chocolate, strawberry, and fresh-picked blackberry milkshakes so thick that if you try and drink them from a straw you feel like you might turn your face inside out. Fat Smitty's is a great place to go anytime you are in the Discovery Bay area, but you can only imagine how good that food tastes after hiking in the mountains for any length of time.

So AJ, Scoot, and I were famished as we walked into Fat Smitty's that particular Saturday afternoon. As the waitress sat us down and handed us each a menu, we looked around the crowded room to soak in our surroundings. This was the first time AJ's dad

7-17 17-6 20 5-8 14-2 3-3 13-3 4-6 12-10 5-22 16-15 1-27 had ever been to Fat Smitty's, and all he could say was, "Oh wow," every five seconds. The three of us laughed. Mr. Seeva was as entertaining as anything tacked to the walls or ceiling.

As our laughter subsided and the others began to look at their menus, I kept looking around the room because I already knew what I wanted to order. I froze. My heart leapt into my throat. Just a couple tables away sat the most beautiful red-headed girl I had ever seen. Well, not that I had *ever* seen, because I had actually seen her before. She was a ninth-grader at our junior high. Her name was Arwen McIntyre.

I discovered how cute Arwen was when we got our yearbooks the last couple weeks of school. As I riffled through the pages of pictures and memories of the school year, I saw her standing next to my sister Tamara in the Jazz Choir photo. Boy, was I regretting my decision to skip out on all of my sister's choir festivals. Anyway, I had spent the last weeks of school trying to "bump into" Arwen in the halls between classes—even risking being late to my own classes—but I never once saw her up close.

But now, here she was, sitting just a couple tables away from me! I looked over at AJ and Scooter. They both had their heads buried in the menus, discussing their upcoming order selections. I looked back at Arwen, she was sitting at a table with a man I guessed was her dad. I didn't really wonder why they were there. I mean, there are plenty of fun activities to do up in Port Angeles or at Hurricane

6-12 10-4 3-4 8-11 1-9 11-2 13-17 28-7 24-10 4-1 7-2 7-3

Ridge, and Fat Smitty's is an awesome place to have lunch on the way. But Arwen and her dad didn't look like they were having fun. It was hard to hear anything in the crowded restaurant, but her dad's body language clearly showed that he was angry. And Arwen appeared to be the focus of that anger. Her head was down, and it looked as if she may have been crying. And she was still beautiful.

She looked up, and our eyes met. I flashed her a smile and she returned a half-smile. In her eyes grew a look of recognition, and then that half-smile turned into a full grin. She recognized me! That's a good thing, right? *Woohoo*, I thought. *She knows I exist!* Just then, it seemed her father said something to her in a harsh tone of voice, and she quickly looked away from me in embarrassment.

The waitress came and took our order, and then we talked for awhile about all the fish we had seen in the lake while on our hike and how we had wished we had brought some fishing gear. Then our burgers and shakes arrived, and all conversations took a backseat to trying to get the mammoth burgers in our mouths. The whole time this was going on, I kept stealing glances at Arwen, and every so often she would look up at the same time and we would both smile and look away.

After awhile Mr. McIntyre stood up, and I watched as he walked past our table headed toward the restroom. I turned back towards Arwen, and she was staring right at me! She smiled and then took

4-1 8-8 3-15 7-2 11-4 7-9 15-5 16-4 14 13-15 3-13 1-5

a napkin and starting writing on it with a pen that she found lying on the table. I looked to see if anyone else was seeing what I was seeing, but Scooter and Mr. Seeva had their backs turned to Arwen's table and AJ was too distracted trying to squeeze his milkshake through his tiny straw. He looked like a little kid doing a fish impression. I looked back at Arwen. As she finished writing, she held up the napkin and pointed at me! The she took the napkin, folded it up, and stuffed it among the dollars tacked to the wall next to her. She looked at me again and smiled.

Suddenly, her smile melted into sadness. Just then her father brushed past me on his way back from the restroom, and I then understood why her expression had changed so quickly. He must have said it was time to go because he didn't even sit back down. He just grabbed his jacket off the back of his chair and started to walk out. Arwen got up, shot me one last look, and then turned and followed her dad out of the restaurant.

Once she was gone, I knew I could not wait long to grab the napkin she had placed on the wall. I was sure it was some kind of message for me. The busboy would be by to clean the table soon, and as busy as Fat Smitty's was, more people would be sitting down right away. So I just stood up, walked over to her table, grabbed the napkin as if I had left the note there and then changed my mind, and then stuffed the napkin in my pocket as I went back to my table.

5-5 13-6 17-2 16-8 4-4 2-20 8-8 16-13 10-9 18-7 4-3 1-19

Scooter gave me an inquisitive look. I thought I would get lucky and he wouldn't say anything, but the second Mr. Seeva got up to use the restroom, Scooter was on my case. "What was that all about?" Scooter asked.

I tried to play dumb: "What was what all about?" It didn't work.

"That napkin you plucked off the wall," Scooter said. He apparently had turned around to see what I was doing when I had gotten up.

"Well, you didn't see who was sitting at that table," I said.

"Yeah, so?" Scooter replied.

"Was it someone famous?" AJ asked. "Are you keeping their napkin as a souvenir? That's a little creepy, don't you think?"

"No, it wasn't someone famous. It was a girl named Arwen from school."

Scooter frowned. "That girl who just left the restaurant a minute ago? I would have thought I'd have recognized her if she went to our school."

"Wait!" AJ interjected. "Let me get this straight. You kept a napkin from a girl, and she is not famous? That's even more creepy!"

"She was in ninth grade last year along with my sister, Tamara. That's why you probably didn't recognize her." I began unfolding the napkin so I could read the message, "And I was not keeping a souvenir napkin! She wrote me a note."

I read the note quickly. It read, "Hey! Please call

2-2 9-21 2-9 7-3 12-4 6-1 7-11 15-3 5-5 4-4

me!" and then it listed her number. I couldn't help but grin from ear to ear: Arwen wanted me to call her! I handed the note across the table for Scooter to read.

"Call her, huh? How do you know that note is from her? How do you know it was intended for you?" Scooter was skeptical.

"Because I watched her write it, doofus! And she looked right at me when she put it on the wall." But inside I started to have this nagging feeling of doubt. What if she wasn't actually looking at me but at someone *behind* me? I quickly turned around to see who was sitting behind me, but all that was there was the dollar-covered hallway to the bathroom. No, I was right: she was leaving that message for me and only me!

The rest of the meal was sort of a blur. Mr. Seeva returned from the bathroom and went back to attacking his burger, while AJ and Scooter continued to harass me about the napkin by shooting me funny looks every chance they got. But I didn't care. Arwen wanted me to call her, and that's what I was thinking about. In fact I figured I would call her from our headquarters when we got back into town, and the boys could listen in while I got the last laugh!

9-14 14-2 17-15 10-5 9-7 11-5 3-1 4-2 13-3 14-3 9-1 9-26

CHAPTER 2

Devastating Developments

The ride home dragged on and on. What should have been a quick forty-minute drive ended up being more like two hours. On the way home we had to cross the Hood Canal Bridge, which actually floats on the water. It is pretty neat to drive across. It's like a drawbridge: if a boat needs to get through, they close the bridge. But instead of raising a section of the bridge for the boat to pass, an entire section of bridge gets moved to the side. That day there was a submarine on the surface of the water, and it needed to pass through the bridge. It was sporting a Canadian flag, and a bunch of sailors were standing on top of the submarine as it passed by. I didn't even know Canada had a navy! Who knows, maybe that day I saw most of it! Anyway, on a normal day that would have been a pretty cool sight to see, but all I could think about was getting home and calling Arwen. After the boat passed through the bridge, it took another fifteen minutes before the bridge section was put back in place. Like I said, the ride home seemed to take an eternity.

It was well past three in the afternoon when we got home. Normally I would be ready to just sack out on the couch and watch some cartoons until dinner, but I had a point to prove and a phone call to make. I told my mom I would be back in time for dinner, and then I headed over to AJ's house. My mom didn't have a lot of rules for me during the summer. I could pretty much come and go as I pleased, but she was pretty insistent that I be at dinner every night at six unless I called to make other arrangements.

I could have taken the trail through the woods behind our houses to get to AJ's. But I'd had enough hiking on trails for one weekend, so I hopped on my bike, even though it was a very short ride. When I got to his house, the garage door was up, and AJ was putting away his camping stuff on the shelves lining the walls.

"AJ, I gotta make a phone call to a girl who lost her napkin. Care to join me?" I said with a smirk.

"Sure, Ty, I'm always up for a little entertainment. Heading over to HQ? I'll meet you over there."

"Yeah," I said as I turned my bike around and headed back down the driveway toward Scooter's house.

HQ, as we have come to know it by now, is the headquarters for the Enigma Squad. It is located in Scooter's backyard. Or I should say *under* Scooter's backyard. Back when they built Scooter's house, they

4-7 13-2 6-4 12-9 19-6 15-15 11-2 3-1 1-2 11-8 6-7 12-5

put a bomb shelter underground behind his house. The only entrance was what looked like a manhole cover in the ground. Over the years, the blackberry bushes in the backyard had grown over the top of the cover, and the owners must have forgotten about it. When they sold the house to Scooter's family, they somehow forgot to tell the new owners they had a bomb shelter in the backyard.

Scooter, AJ, and I accidently found the shelter while fetching a football out of the blackberries, and we have been using it as the secret base of operations for the Enigma Squad just about ever since. Only a handful of adults even know we have this headquarters, and part of our mission is to keep it that way. As you will soon find out, actually keeping HQ a secret would require much more work than we were expecting.

When I got to Scooter's house, I parked my bike in his driveway and was just about to ring the doorbell when the front door flew open. Out jumped Scooter, nearly tackling me.

"Don't ring the doorbell!" he whispered. "Urpy finally fell asleep. He has been fighting a nap all afternoon, and the nap finally won!"

Urpy is Scooter's three-year-old little brother. His real name is Wyatt, but we call him Urpy, which is our version of Earp. If you didn't know, Wyatt Earp was a famous cowboy, and little Wyatt Parks was making gun sounds as soon as he was able to make noise with his mouth, so the nickname seemed appropriate.

6-3 19-1 13-1 5-9 3-5 5-3 12-4 9-3 17-1 15-2 9-4 2-9

"So I thought we could head down to HQ and call Arwen. I'll prove to you guys once and for all that this napkin was meant for me. AJ is on his way. Are you in?"

"Yeah, sure." He quietly shut the front door behind him. "But let's go around."

We walked around the house into the backyard, where we junior-highers love to play football after school. Beyond the manicured grass lawn are some madrone and fir trees. We walked into the woods and then took a left and walked straight towards the blackberry bushes that were creeping out from the greenbelt—the bushes and trees between Scooter's house and his neighbor Jimmy Langsworth's.

When we reached the blackberries, Scooter reached inside them, pushed a stick to the side, and then pulled. With little effort, a door made entirely of blackberries swung open to reveal a tunnel leading into the thorny bushes. We both crouched inside and then pulled the camouflage door shut behind us and latched it. We call this tunnel the Right Hook, because as you exit, it is actually a right turn off a larger main tunnel, which runs straight along the greenbelt.

"I imagine AJ will be coming in the Straight-a-Way, don't you think?" Scooter asked, explaining why he was closing the blackberry door behind us. The Straight-a-Way is the name we gave the main tunnel. The tunnels gave us two entrances and exits from the blackberry bushes that hid our HQ. We

4-2 10-4 18-5 8-13 9-9 3-14 16-2 10-1 9-7 2-4 8-4 12-13

were working on cutting a third—the Emergency Exit—which went directly west and would come out in the Langsworths' yard. But we hadn't figured out how to hide the entrance yet, so that project had been put on hold for now. We crawled down the Right Hook until it joined up with the Straight-a-Way and then crouched and hobbled the rest of the way to the metal plate in the ground, which is the entrance to the bomb shelter. I haven't come up with a good name for what to call that form of walking that we do in the tunnel. The tunnel is big enough that you don't have to crawl on your hands and knees, but it is short enough that you can't stand upright and walk either. Maybe I should call it a squat-walk. Whatever it is, I am glad nobody else can see us moving through the blackberries, because I am sure we look ridiculous.

Well, back to the metal plate. Directly underneath is a simple room with a ladder and a vault door similar to the kind you would find in a bank. That door leads into the actual bomb shelter and our headquarters. As we lifted the lid and went down the ladder, we could see that the vault door was already open, which meant AJ must have arrived moments before us. In order to have beaten us to HQ, he must have taken the shortcut from his house through the woods behind Scooter's house.

As we walked through the doorway, AJ was leaning against the refrigerator, eating an apple. Scooter felt it was necessary to give AJ a hard time about leaving the door open. "Oh, don't worry, AJ, we have our keys. You don't have to leave the door open for us!"

Amazingly enough, AJ picked up on Scooter's sarcasm. "What!" he said. "I knew you guys would be right behind me!"

"Well, if that is the case, why not just prop the metal lid up for us then?" Scooter snapped.

"Hold on, Scoot, that's totally different..." AJ stammered.

"Isn't that a bit of an overreaction there, Scoot?" I added.

"Guys, I don't think you get it. HQ is a key part of the Enigma Squad. I have my computer down here now. Plus the cash box! There's not a lot in it yet, but there will be!"

"Relax, Scooter," AJ said. "Besides, that's why you installed all those new security features, right?"

"Yes, but I have not gotten a chance to test them out yet!" If only he knew how quickly he would get that chance.

"Okay, I am sorry for leaving the door open..." AJ apologized, "...for two minutes!"

"Thank you!" Scooter said, letting the sarcasm slide as he plopped himself down on the futon couch.

So I know what you're thinking. A futon? A fridge? A computer? What kind of a bomb shelter is this? Well, the sweetest kind possible, I'd say! Our little HQ has a full-sized fridge, a futon that turns into a couch or a bed, a small table, a phone, a sink, and even a toilet! I guess whoever built the bomb shelter thought they would be underground for a long time. How the furniture got down there is a long story, though, so I'll just say I am grateful we found it that way. Since we found it, we have pretty much left the place as-is except for the fact that Scooter hooked up his computer down there. Oh, and he also took some old curtains his mom was getting rid of and hung them from the ceiling to give a little bit of privacy to whoever needed to use the toilet. He got the idea from seeing those curtains that split a hospital room in two. Luckily, the curtains have not been used yet because we also made a rule that the toilet was to be used only in extreme emergencies, and we haven't had one of those yet.

AJ finished his apple and began what I figured would be endless harassment of me. "So, Ty, are you going to call this napkin friend of yours or what?"

Scooter laughed out loud.

Oh, don't encourage him, Scooter! I thought to myself. "Her name is Arwen, and yes, I am going to call her right now."

"Make sure to initiate 'Surround Speak,'" Scooter reminded me. Scooter had rigged the landline phone to run through the computer. He had also found some free software that made the phone use the computer's speakers as a sort of speakerphone. This way, all three of us could hear what was being said when we made phone calls. That's why I wanted to make the phone call to Arwen from down in HQ. Otherwise, Scooter and AJ would never believe my version of what was said when I called her.

I pulled the napkin with Arwen's phone number out of my pocket and dialed the number. AJ sat down, and he and Scooter leaned back on the couch, obviously preparing to laugh as quietly as possible. The phone rang a couple times before a woman answered.

"Hello, McIntyre residence." I thought this must be Arwen's mom.

"Uh, hello. Is Arwen there?" I said a little nervously.

"She is. May I ask who is calling?"

"This is Tyler Pate. I'm a friend from school." I guess that was sort of true.

"Sure. Please hold."

A few very long seconds passed before Arwen picked up the phone. "Hey, Tyler, I am so glad you called! I guess you got my message."

My heart jumped. I couldn't help but smile. I turned toward Scooter and AJ and flashed them my best I-told-you-so smirk. "Yes I did, Arwen. I am so glad you wanted me to call you. I was thinking maybe I should call you even before I got your note."

"You, you were?" Arwen sounded surprised. "Oh. Uh, well anyway, I wanted to talk to you about something…"

"Yes?" I said excitedly. I couldn't believe this was actually happening. And my two best friends were there to see it happen.

"Yeah, I remember seeing the newspaper article in the *Ridgetop Round-up* about you and your friends solving some crime in Canada right before school let out for the summer. You guys are regular heroes!" Arwen was referring to our junior high's newspaper. Near the end of the school year, the newspaper did a big article on how we solved *The Case of the Old Man in the Mailbox*. It had an extensive interview with Scooter and then a cool picture of the three of us getting an award from Commander Coleman of the Silverdale Police. Apparently the good press helped Arwen, a ninth-grader, notice this seventh-grader. It sounded like she had some of the details of that case mixed up, but hey, who cares!

"Gee, thanks, Arwen, but we were just doing our jobs." I tried to sound humble. "We were just glad we could help."

"Well, great! That's what I wanted to talk to you about. I want to hire you guys!"

What?! That's why she wanted to talk to me? To hire us? I thought it was for... Oh, I was so mistaken! I looked over at AJ—he was doubled over in laughter and trying to do it quietly. I could feel the blood rushing to my face; I was so embarrassed.

"Oh," was all I could manage to say at first. I know I probably sounded disappointed. "You, you want to hire us, huh? Well, what for?"

"Well, I live in the Eagle Vista Apartments and—"

"Ah, the old Birdcage, huh?" I interrupted. The Eagle Vista Apartment complex is just down the hill from the housing development that AJ, Scoot, and I live in. We have quite a few friends from school who live in those apartments. All the streets within the complex are named after birds, like Pelican Place, Seagull Street, Albatross Avenue, you get the picture. Anyway, we always used to forget exactly what the apartment complex was called, so awhile back, I just nicknamed the whole place "the Birdcage." Our friends who live there thought it was pretty catchy, and now all the kids refer to those apartments as the Birdcage.

"Uh yeah, the Birdcage," she chuckled. Then she continued, "So anyway, the other day my friend Diedra and I were on our mountain bikes, and we went up the hill to the clubhouse to buy a soda from one of the machines, so we left our bikes out front for like five minutes, tops. Then we came back out and rolled back down the hill to my apartment, but when I went to hit the brakes, the cable snapped, and I couldn't stop, and I crashed into my dad's pickup truck. I put a huge dent in the door, and my dad was royally ticked off! Then right before we got to the burger place, he got a call from the repair shop, and he found out it's going to cost like $3500 to get the truck fixed. That's why he was so mad when you saw us!"

"Oh, wow. I am sorry to hear that Arwen, but I'm confused why you need to hire us."

"Because it wasn't my fault! Like I said, the brakes didn't work. The brake cable completely snapped!"

6-3 14-7 18-3 8-8 2-2 6-6 16-16 6 13-9 11-6 17-6 3-9

"Could the brakes have just worn out?" I asked.

"No! And that's the thing: my bike is almost brand new. I got it for my birthday only two weeks ago. That's the other reason my dad is mad. He thinks I must not have been taking care of my bike for it to break down so soon."

"Well, then what do you think happened?"

"I think someone messed with my bike."

"Really? You think someone cut your brake cable?"

"I don't know. That's why I want to hire you guys. I looked at the cable, and it doesn't look worn, and it doesn't look like a cut either—it almost looks like some sort of a burn mark."

"A burn mark? Wow!" I exclaimed. "Is there someone you suspect could have done this?"

"I don't know. I thought everybody liked me! But when we went up to the clubhouse to get our soda, there were a bunch of guys walking past to go play basketball on the court nearby. I thought maybe one of them could have done it. After all, my brakes stopped working *after* we went inside."

"Yeah, sounds suspicious," I agreed. "Well, it sounds like you just might have a case. Let me talk to Scooter and AJ and see what they think."

I looked over at both of them across the room. AJ was nodding emphatically, and Scooter was wearing his "thinking face," his signature half-grin, half-frown. I could see he was already processing the few clues we were given so far. He was hooked.

4-1 10-2 1-19 13-4 19-2 16-6 6-10 12-3 3-1 58

I tried to pour on the charm, "You know what? I don't even need to confer with them. I am just going to say that we will take the case, and those guys will have to get on board later."

AJ rolled his eyes. He knew I was just kissing up to Arwen, but I didn't care. She may have wanted me to call her so she could hire us, but I was going to use that time to my advantage and charm her in the process.

"That's great, Tyler! And I actually have someone who could help you—my little sister, Traverna. She will be going into the seventh grade next year, but she is super-smart. I know she will be a big help to you. She could probably solve this case on her own, but, well, she would probably just do better if she was helping someone instead of digging into things by herself."

Ugh, I thought to myself. *A girl as part of the Enigma Squad? No, thank you.* I looked at AJ and Scooter; they were both shaking their heads. They also thought it was a bad idea.

"Uh, Arwen, I think we will pass. We sort of have our own process… and we like to work alone."

"But she would be a big help. Like I said—"

"Really, Arwen," I interrupted. "We will be fine. Honest."

"Okay… But Traverna has already started digging into the case, so your paths might cross somewhere along the way."

"That's fine. I am sure it will be okay," I answered.

3-18 14-1 11-7 7-2 5-18 8-3 9-2 2-3 7-9 4-4 16-9 16-9

"So where will you guys start?" she said, wrapping up the phone conversation.

"Well, I will have to talk to the guys, but I am guessing we will want to take a look at your bike first." I looked toward Scooter who was nodding his head in agreement. "I will call you again, and we can set a time to come down there to the Birdcage and take a look around too."

"Sounds great, Tyler. Thank you so much for taking this case." Her voice sounded so sweet just then. My heart melted.

"No problem, anytime," I said. "I am just glad I—"

I did not get to finish my thought; she had hung up the phone. AJ and Scooter could not hold in their laughter any longer, and they made an exaggerated point of laughing as loudly as they could for a good thirty seconds.

"Ty, I stand corrected. You were right: that napkin really was meant for you!" AJ could not resist giving me a hard time. I had to admit, Arwen's intentions were much different than I had thought they were, but I was determined to get the last laugh on this one. I was going to solve this case and win her heart.

The next day was going to be Sunday, and Scooter and his family had plans to visit his uncle's church over in Seattle. So the three of us agreed to get together on Monday at HQ and then head down to the Birdcage to check out Arwen's bike. Then, mostly because I wanted a hot shower before dinner (but

8 7-2 12-1 6-4 11-7 1-4 6-10 7-1 9-10 5-3 9-1 2-12

partially out of embarrassment over the whole situation), I told the guys I had to get home. With a little more ribbing from AJ, they let me leave.

2-5 1-17 3-14 3-21 1-22 17

CHAPTER 3

Three is Company, Four is a Crowd

Monday morning, I woke up really late. Mom was out running errands, and my sister was sitting at the kitchen table reading some magazine. AJ called me to say he was on his way over to HQ, and I figured he had called Scooter as well. I needed a quick breakfast, so I took a banana out of the fruit bowl. Then, despite Tamara's protests, I also grabbed a handful of cereal out of a box from the cupboard, stuffed it in my mouth, and plopped the box down on the kitchen table before I walked out the front door. I took the shortcut through the woods to Scooter's house and HQ. As I climbed down the ladder and closed the lid above me, the outer room to HQ became pitch black. Luckily, Scooter had realized this would be a problem, and so at the bottom of the ladder, he had attached to the wall one of those dome lights that you just push and the whole dome lights up. It works great. Not only does it light up the whole room, but even when you have your hands full, it is easy to turn on by nudging it with your elbow. If you have ever tried to flick on a light switch with your elbow, you know what a great invention those dome light things are! With the room lit up by the single light, I could easily see the bank-vault door in the opposite wall. I pulled my copy of the key out of my pocket and put it in the keyhole, pushed the handle down, and heaved the large door open.

To my surprise, both AJ and Scooter were already inside the room. AJ, as usual, was eating something—this resembled chocolate pudding—and Scooter was typing away on his computer keyboard. I wasn't surprised to see Scooter on his computer, and I certainly was not surprised to find AJ eating. No, what surprised me was that the door was shut when they knew I was coming. Apparently, Scooter's little lecture about keeping the door closed had worked.

I closed the door behind me, and Scooter looked up from his computer.

"Hey, Ty! You ready to go solve our next case?"

"You bet!" I said, tossing my empty banana peel into the trash. "You got what you need? I am just going to call Arwen and tell her to be expecting us."

I grabbed the phone off the small bookshelf next to the computer and started dialing. I tried to hurry so AJ would not have an opportunity to harass me and Scoot would not have time to turn on the Surround Speak. I was in no mood for more teasing, so I decided to keep this conversation semi-private.

9-3 14-1 9-18 15-5 4-8 7-4 1-3 5-2 13-10 17-1 4-12 12-4

Arwen answered the phone and informed me that today would not be a good day to stop by because she was about to walk out the door to attend Cheer mini-camp at the high school for the day. But she said she was glad I called because she wanted me to know what she had heard. Apparently, she had just found out about a girl from the other side of the Birdcage, whose brand-new bike had lost its brakes on Sunday. Arwen had only heard about it, so the details were very fuzzy. But the story she told sounded very similar to her own.

Once again, she told me her little sister was already running down new leads on the case and that we should have her join our investigation. Once again, I refused.

I hung up the phone and filled the guys in on what was said on the phone.

AJ chimed in first. "So what do we do now? We obviously can't go down to the apartments if Arwen is not going to be there!"

"It sounds like a great morning for some research, then," Scooter answered. "I am guessing that it is not a coincidence that two bikes had their brakes fail in the same week in the same neighborhood. That lends some validity to my hypothesis that the bikes were tampered with."

AJ looked confused. "Validity to the hypo-what-the-sis?"

Scooter rolled his eyes. "Something sounds suspicious, is what I am saying. I think it is rather unlikely that two bikes just happened to break on their own. I think they had a little help."

"Oh," AJ nodded. "So how do we prove it?"

"Well, since we can't go look at the bikes today, we can see if there have been any other bikes that have broken," Scooter said.

"Let's check the police section of the online newspapers," I suggested. "See if there have been any reports filed with the police in recent weeks."

"Exactly what I was thinking," Scooter said. "And maybe tomorrow we can interview some other neighbors and see if they have seen or heard anything."

Scooter pulled up a search engine on the computer and began typing away. We spent the next twenty minutes or so looking at the last few weeks of newspapers, searching for any mention of stolen or damaged bicycles.

Just as we were really getting into a groove with our newspaper research, the overhead lights in the shelter went out. My heart skipped a beat, and AJ started whining, "Oh great, now the power went out!"

The room was still fairly lit by the computer screen. I had to laugh at AJ. "If the power went out, then why did the computer stay on?" I asked.

Scooter began to whisper. "The lights did not go out because of a power outage; the lights went out as part of my new security measures. We are now on intruder alert!"

5-4 7-1 4-9 10-2 18-5 4-6 4-3 4-4 8-12 9-1 18

Now I was panicking—all the thoughts of being stuck underground with no way of getting out came rushing over me. I just imagined some fat intruder sitting on top of our only exit, the metal lid. Scooter interrupted my panic attack, and calmly began to explain his new little alarm system.

It all started with Mr. Greeley. Mr. Greeley lives several doors down from Scooter, and I am guessing he is in his mid-sixties. Apparently, Mr. Greeley had some problems with raccoons getting into his trash cans at night, so he installed some motion-sensor lights above the trash cans. Whenever the raccoons came near, his hope was that the sensors would sense their movement, and the lights would turn on and scare the critters away. Well, Mr. Greeley must have somehow installed the lights backward or something because the lights always stayed on until the raccoons came around, and then when the motion sensors detected them, the lights would turn off! It was exactly the opposite of what he intended.

Mr. Greeley thought the whole apparatus was defective, so he bought some new motion detectors to install. But this time he called Scooter's dad to see if he could help him install them. He knew that Mr. Parks was an engineer. Scooter heard about the dilemma and decided to tag along and help. It wasn't until after installing the new lights that Mr. Greeley realized there was nothing wrong with the first set of lights. He had just installed them incorrectly. Mr. Greeley was just going to throw away

7-1 14-4 16-6 18-10 11-1 10-3 1-4 7-4 7-5 6-12 13-8 34

the old motion-sensors, since he figured he couldn't return them now that they were used, but Scooter asked if he could keep them instead. Scooter took them into his backyard, and with a little help from his dad, Scooter set up the motion detectors near the edge of the blackberries and near the trails in the woods. Then like Mr. Greeley had done on accident, he *purposefully* hooked up the sensors backwards to the lights in the shelter. That way when the sensors were triggered by movement anywhere near our secret hideout, the lights would go out inside HQ. *Pretty cool,* I thought. Now, if anyone got anywhere near the entrances to the tunnels in the blackberries, we would know about it. Apparently Scooter had just finished hooking everything up that morning. I guess they worked!

Scooter finished his story about the alarm setup, and then we shuffled out the vault door and huddled at the base of the ladder. Scooter reached down to the ground at the base of the ladder and grabbed a piece of pipe, which was about one inch thick, bent sort of in the shape of an S. I recognized it as a periscope he had made for a school project last year. Inside the pipe were a couple different mirrors set at different angles so if you looked through one end of the pipe, you could see out the other end, even though the pipe had two sharp bends in it.

"Let's see who our visitor is, shall we?" he said.

He tucked the pipe under his arm and then climbed up the ladder until his head was ready to

10-16 4-5 17-2 13-3 5-1 2-10 11-8 3-13 1-5 6-4 10-3 3

hit the metal plate above him. With one hand holding onto the ladder for balance, he grabbed the pipe
with the other. At the top of the ladder, he used his
head to turn the handle on the underside of the lid
and then pushed up the metal lid ever so slowly.
When the lid was open about an inch and a half,
Scooter slid one end of the pipe out of the opening
and then closed the lid so it was pinching the pipe
in the opening. Then he descended a couple rungs
on the ladder until the other end of the pipe was
at about eye level. Ta-da! He could now look in his
periscope and see what was going on outside.

Scooter was quiet for a few moments as he turned
the pipe a little in each direction to get a wider view.
He climbed back down the ladder and left the pipe
hanging from the lid, still stuck out of the opening.
"It is hard to see that well through all the blackberries, but it looks like there is some girl wandering
around my backyard, right near the edge of the
woods. She looks like she may be lost. Let's give her
a sec, maybe she will just wander away the same
way she wandered in."

"I wanna see," AJ muttered, climbing up the ladder. He too looked into the periscope. After only a
couple seconds, he slid down the rails of the ladder and then whispered more quietly than before:
"She's not going away! In fact she's right by the
blackberries!"

I had a brilliant thought. "Why don't you go back
inside HQ and call your mom, Scoot? Give her some

12-1 4-3 11-6 7-9 6-1 19-2 9-10 2-3 1-1 17-2 15

reason to look outside in the backyard. Once she sees the girl, you know she will do something."

"I got an even better idea, Ty! It's time to use my new Distraction Device."

"Your what?" AJ and I whispered practically in unison.

"Well, that's the other part of my new security system: detect and distract. Remember when Jimmy from next door put that new fancy alarm system into his Camaro, so anytime you get near his car, it starts talking to you and telling you to 'step away from the car'?"

"Yeah," AJ and I chuckled at his sorry excuse for a robot impersonation.

"Well, when he installed the new alarm, he threw away the old one. I dug through his garbage and found all the parts and put them to good use. I took the little speaker that makes the siren noise, and I put it in plastic and then attached it to the inside of the rainspout on the corner of my house. And here—" He pulled a key chain out of his pocket. "—is the alarm button."

AJ looked a little puzzled. Admittedly, I was *almost* as clueless as he was.

"So, let's all get ready to get out of here," Scooter whispered. "I will climb up and look out the periscope. When I think the time is right, I will push the button, and the car alarm ought to scare her silly. Hopefully she either runs away or at least walks toward the house and the noise. While her back is turned, we will all get out of here and quietly head down the Straight-a-Way tunnel. Then, we circle back as if we had just come from way back in the woods."

"Great," I said.

"Perfect!" AJ added.

Scooter scrambled up the ladder, and after only a couple seconds of looking in the periscope, he pushed the *PANIC* button on the key chain. Even down underground, we could easily hear the sound of the car alarm. Scooter continued to look through the periscope for a few more seconds, and then he pulled the pipe out of the opening and opened the lid all the way. He handed the periscope pipe to AJ, who was halfway up the ladder, who then handed it to me. I set it down quietly on the floor and then quickly scrambled up the ladder and closed the lid behind me. Scooter was watching the house and silently motioned for me to keep moving. He followed with his back to me so he could watch our rear.

We safely and quietly made it all the way to the end of the Straight-a-Way and then closed the camouflage door. Scooter suggested we run back to the house to make it look like we had heard an alarm while playing in the woods and it had caused us to come running. As we came out of the woods and into the backyard, Scooter hit the *PANIC* button again, and the alarm stopped.

I don't think what we saw next was part of

5-2 16-6 30-22 12-8 9-5 3-7 11-2 18-8 21-1 5-5 1

Scooter's distraction plan. The girl Scooter had tried to scare off was standing on his back porch. Standing next to her, with hands on hips, was Scooter's mom, and she did not look happy!

"Sean, what in the world was that noise?" Mrs. Parks asked.

Thinking fast, I spoke up. "Sorry, Mrs. P! Scooter, AJ, and me were just trying to set up an alarm system for the backyard. We didn't realize it would be so loud."

"You mean, 'Scooter, AJ, *and I*'?"

I looked at my friends in confusion. "Yeah, that's what I just said."

"No, you said, 'Scooter, AJ, and *me*.' That is incorrect. It should be, 'Scooter, AJ, and I,'" she corrected me.

Embarrassed, I looked around for someone to bail me out, but no help was coming. "Uh, yeah, that's what I meant."

Mrs. Parks gave me a stern look. "Then I suggest you say what you mean." Her look softened then, and she gave me a half-grin. I see now where Scooter gets it from.

"All right," I said, raising my hands in joking surrender. "The three of us were working on an alarm system for the backyard."

The girl on the porch spoke up for the first time. "I'd say it worked! You scared the loving sunlight out of me!"

Mrs. Parks, trying her best to hide her confusion

12-1 4-4 2-5 19-5 9-11 3-7 15-3 17-4 2-6 7-1 12-6 6-3

as to what that meant, spoke up. "Well, boys, your system is going to need some work to distinguish between friend and enemy, then. This is Traverna Lynn. She says she is here to help you with your latest case. I did not realize you boys had a new case, but I sent her along to the backyard, where I thought you were playing. The next thing I know, a car alarm is going off in the backyard, and the only person I see there is poor Traverna Lynn, wondering what just happened!"

"Yeah, sorry, Mom. We weren't expecting company," Scooter apologized. "How did you find us anyway, Traverna?"

"Please call me Traverna Lynn."

"Um, okay. So how did you know where I lived, Traverna Lynn?"

"Simple. My sister, Arwen, is friends with Tyler's sister, Tamara, and so she dropped me off at the Pates' house on her way to Cheer camp. She thought maybe I could help you guys on your case." She pointed at me. "You were obviously not home, but Tamara told me Scooter lived just down the street, so I came over here. Easy as cake!"

"Don't you mean 'pie'?" AJ chuckled.

"Oh, right," she said. "It was a piece of pie!"

Mrs. Parks jumped in. "Well, it sounds like we all have a lot to talk about. I was just about to fix Wyatt a grilled cheese sandwich and tomato soup. I am sure I have enough bread for everyone. Why don't we have lunch and continue this talk?"

5 12-2 16-7 18-2 1-1 6-1 9-7 8-1 2-9 2-13 4-8 5

You didn't have to tell AJ twice; he was practically inside the house before she was finished with the invite. The rest of us followed.

Traverna Lynn and the three of us boys sat down at the table and started talking while Mrs. Parks worked her magic in the kitchen. Urpy began running his toy cars up and down everyone's shoulders as he worked his way around the dining room table.

"So your sister sent you up here, huh?" Scooter asked.

"Yeah, I was about to go out and talk to the neighbor kids about the bikes belonging to Arwen and this other girl, Brooklyn, but she didn't think that was such a good idea. So she suggested I come up here and we might be able to help each other."

AJ leaned over to me and whispered, "Your napkin girlfriend is pretty pushy, don't you think?"

"Shut up," I whispered back. But he was right. Arwen was really pushing hard for us to work with this kid.

"Is Brooklyn the girl with the bike that broke after your sister's?" Scooter asked Traverna Lynn.

"Yeah. She lives on the other side of the apartments." She took her hat off and placed it on the table, then ran her hand through her short, curly blond hair. She had a bad case of hat hair, but I guessed that her hair was always messed up, whether she wore a hat or not. She sort of gave me the impression that she didn't concern herself with looks very much.

5-1 7-3 17-3 6-11 12-1 3-6 5-9 20-7 16-5 1-1 78

What with the intruder alert, the car alarm, and the run through the woods, my adrenaline was pumping too hard earlier to notice much about Traverna Lynn. But now that we were just sitting at the table across from each other, I began to really take note of what she looked like. She seemed to have her own sense of style. I am not up on ladies' fashion or anything, but the name on her pink T-shirt was not one I had ever heard of. Her blue jeans had holes in all the right places, indicating the jeans had earned those holes from playing hard, as opposed to being bought that way. (I still can't believe people actually buy jeans with holes already in them!) Finally, I noticed her shoes. They were camouflage green with just a splash of pink to remind you they were girl shoes. Based on the wear and tear on her shoes and the overall style of her entire outfit, I guessed she liked to skateboard.

"So do you like to skateboard, Traverna Lynn?" I asked.

"Oh yeah, I actually brought mine with me. Should make the trip back down to my house much better than walking."

"Do you know any cool tricks?" AJ asked.

"Some. I practice every chance I get, as long as my mom isn't watching. It seems like every time I turn around, she is breathing down my throat!"

AJ chuckled. "Don't you mean, 'Breathing down your neck'?" It must have given him a thrill to be the one actually correcting somebody else for a change.

3-4 8-1 14-3 10-11 7-16 2-6 11-5 13-1 16-5 19-2 1-13 5

"Sure, whatever," she said.

While we were all laughing, Mrs. Parks came in from the kitchen with a plate stacked high with grilled cheese sandwiches. "There is tomato soup in a pot on the stove for any and all who want some. And, Tyler, the ketchup is in the door of the fridge, as usual." She rolled her eyes at me as she sat down next to Urpy to cheerlead his lunch intake.

Scooter's mom was rolling her eyes at me because of a previous discussion we'd had about the proper way to eat grilled cheese sandwiches. I grew up dipping my sandwich in ketchup, and well, let's just say I don't believe ketchup and tomato soup are even close to the same thing.

Well, not long into the meal, Urpy started throwing a fit. He refused to eat the sandwich that was sitting on his small plastic plate. "It's too big!" he whined.

Mrs. Parks argued that his sandwich was the exact same size as he normally eats, but he just kept on whining. Finally, Mrs. Parks got up, took his plate, and went into the kitchen. She took a bigger plate out of the cupboard and transferred the sandwich to the bigger plate. Then, she brought the plate in and set it down in front of the three-year-old.

"There, is that better?" she asked.

"Ahh," he exhaled, satisfied. Then he took a huge bite of his sandwich. Parents can be scary smart sometimes.

Near the end of the meal, Traverna Lynn excused

herself to use the bathroom. While she was away, I leaned over to talk to Scooter. "So what do we do now? We can't go back to HQ while Traverna Lynn is here."

"Just send her home," AJ suggested, leaning in from the other side.

"We can't really do that," Scooter countered. "If she tells Arwen we just sent her home, that probably will not earn us much goodwill with our client."

"Yeah, good point," AJ acknowledged.

"I've got it," Scooter said as we straightened up and Traverna Lynn sat back down.

"So, Traverna Lynn, we are thinking about heading into Silverdale and talking to the police. We have a friend on the force, and we thought about seeing if the police have heard of any similar bike stuff happening lately. Would you like to join us?"

"Would I? Of course!"

Then, hoping to maybe deter her, I asked, "So if Scooter, AJ, and me are on our bikes, are you going to be able to keep up on your skateboard?"

"If Scooter, AJ, and *I* are on bikes," Mrs. Parks corrected me. "Tyler, would you say, 'If me am on my bike?' No. You would say, 'If I am on my bike.' So if you add Scooter and AJ to that sentence, it is still I. 'Scooter, AJ, and I.' Just take out the other people, and you'll know which pronoun fits."

"Uh, yeah. Sorry. I got it now."

"I hope so," she said. Then, satisfied with her grammar lesson, she grabbed a few plates off the table and headed into the kitchen.

"Wow! You guys have connections with the police?" Traverna asked after Mrs. Parks had left. "So you guys are the real deal, huh?"

"Yeah, I guess that's why your sister decided to hire us," AJ said proudly.

"That is so cool! I am trying to be a detective myself. In fact, did you guys hear about the graffiti at your junior high on the last day of school? Well, I am going to solve that case before the summer is over."

"I heard about that," AJ said.

"How are you going to solve it?" Scooter asked.

"I have a couple leads I am working on," she said. "We'll just have to see how they work out."

1-6 8-8 12-6 14-17 1-22 5-1 15-28 9-9 3-9 10-2 14-24 6

CHAPTER 4
Beauty in the Birdcage

After lunch, Scooter, AJ, Traverna Lynn, and *I* (see, I am learning, Mrs. P!) left the house and started heading into Silverdale. Once we got to the entrance of our housing development, we got to the fun part of our trip. It is a straight shot all the way to town. The best part is, it is all downhill, for over a mile! It kind of stinks to come back home, because that part of the trip is all uphill. But you can't think about that ahead of time because then you take all the fun out of the five-minute coast down the hill into town.

As we went flying down the road, I took a quick look behind me. I was quite impressed to see that even though we were on bikes and she was on a skateboard, Traverna Lynn was doing a pretty good job of keeping up. She was not far behind at all. I must admit, that girl is braver than I would be. When you are going that fast, standing on a skateboard looks much scarier than riding a bicycle!

About halfway down the hill, we passed the

Birdcage on the left. The apartment complex is surrounded by a wooden fence, with only one road leading in or out. At that entrance is a little guard shack, which is manned by a gruff old man who reads a newspaper for most of the day. He is more of an information desk clerk than a security guard. In fact, cars don't even have to stop at the shack on the way into the complex. Still, I thought perhaps we could talk to the old man on the way back up the hill later. He may remember seeing something suspicious. Besides, I knew I would be huffing and puffing from biking uphill and would probably need a rest at that point anyway.

We flew past the Birdcage, and then shortly afterward, we passed the local skate park on our right. I turned around in time to see Traverna Lynn waving to a few skaters in the park as she flew past.

Later, as the four of us walked into the police station, Commander Coleman was sitting at his desk with a scowl across his face and his nose buried in a file folder. He looked up as we approached his desk. He quickly turned his scowl into a smile and then looked a little confused to see a girl with the three of us boys. Scooter introduced Traverna Lynn to the commander and then explained about Arwen and the damaged bikes. He mentioned how we thought the two bike incidents might be connected and we were wondering if he had heard of any more incidents that may be related.

"I am pretty sure I haven't heard of anything

4-3 13-2 9-4 9-5 12-6 2-5 5-17 7-3 17-3 12-1 12-19 10-7

lately, sorry," Commander Coleman said.

Scooter kept pushing. "Well, do you think you can run a search through your records and verify that?"

"Listen, I appreciate that you boys—and girl—are working so hard on this case, but I have a lot of cases of my own to work on," he said, holding up the file folder he had been reading. "When I get a chance, I'll have an officer run that search for you. But I think I would have remembered any bike crimes."

"Okay, thanks," Scooter said dejectedly.

A little disappointed by the dead-end, we started to leave, but the commander stopped us. "Boys, and Miss McIntyre, I am not sure what you are getting yourselves into, or how big this thing is—if it even is a 'thing'—but I just want to warn you to be careful. You call me directly at the first sign of trouble. I mean it. Remember what happened the last time you got in over your heads." His face turned into a scowl as his eyes tried to burn into our teenage brains that he was serious. He winked and then waved us out the door with his hand as he put his nose back into the file we had pulled him away from.

The trip home took forever because we had to keep waiting on Traverna Lynn and her skateboard. She did a great job of keeping up when we were going downhill, but on the level sidewalks of Silverdale it was another story. Then, as we started up the hill toward home, Traverna Lynn asked if we could stop by the skate park for a second. AJ and

16-3 3-5 5-3 3-9 9-8 8-2 2-7 16-13 12-1 1-7 10-2 9-6

Scooter didn't have a problem with it, and since I was dying from trying to pedal uphill, I was not about to argue. Traverna Lynn said hello to a couple kids she knew, and then after being begged by a couple of the other skaters, she agreed to do "one quick run." She jumped on her skateboard and then dived into the concrete bowl full of jumps and ramps and started doing tricks. She must have been doing some awesome stuff because all the other skaters were going nuts every time she went up into the air, shouting and whooping about her "Frontside 360," "Big Air Stalefish," "Rock to Fakie," and a bunch of other names I am not sure I heard correctly. I don't know anything about skateboarding, but I was still amazed at all the spins and jumps she was doing while never falling off the board. I must admit, this girl was weird, but she was really starting to impress me.

Traverna Lynn eventually jumped out of the concrete bowl, and with a huge smile on her face, she started walking back toward the road to head uphill to her apartment complex. "Hey, guys, thank you so much for letting me shred for a few."

"Are you kidding me? That was awesome!" I said.

"Yeah, I can't believe you can skate like that. We can do this anytime!" AJ exclaimed.

We grinded our way uphill a little farther until we got to the guard shack at the entrance to the Birdcage. Traverna Lynn thought she really needed to get home, so we would have to interview the old man inside the guard shack by ourselves. We agreed we boys would meet at Scooter's house in the morning and then immediately head down to Traverna Lynn's to talk to Arwen and Brooklyn, the other girl with the other broken bicycle. Traverna Lynn thought that Cheer mini-camp was every other day, so she was pretty sure Arwen would be around the next day if we showed up. We said goodbye, and she ran off toward home.

When we interviewed the guard, he didn't have much to add to what we already knew, except to say that since school was out there were a lot more kids running around on bikes and that he was sure "one of them hooligans" would make as good a suspect for mischief as anyone. It was apparent to us that the guard was not a fan of kids, or anyone else who might pull him away from his precious newspaper.

After talking to him and riding up the rest of the dreaded hill to get home, I was pretty much done for the day. I just wanted to get some dinner and then lounge on the couch and make some progress on the library book I had started, *The Hardy Boys: The House on the Cliff*. Ever since starting the Enigma Squad, I'd had a craving for any mystery books I could find.

The next day we met at Scooter's house and then wasted no time getting on our bikes and hitting the road. The ride down the hill to the Birdcage was of course awesome. I even got brave and for a second took both my hands off the handlebars, steering the

5-2 17-8 17-9 8-11 12-1 3-8 7-2 9-1 13-3 6-1 2-4 1-3

bike with my knees. You have to sit up straight in order to pull it off, which makes you slow down a bit, but the thrill is well worth it.

As we slowed down to make the turn into the apartments, we saw that Traverna Lynn was there on her bicycle, talking to the man in the guard shack. As we pulled up, we could hear the guard tell Traverna Lynn that he had answered the same questions yesterday. When the guard saw us approaching, he turned his attention to us. "Is this girl with you?"

"Uh, yes?" I said hesitantly.

"Well, you might want to teach her it isn't a good idea to blame the person you're trying to get information from!" he growled.

"I didn't blame you for anything," Traverna Lynn whined.

"Humph. You all but said that I invited vandals into this complex so that they could destroy your sister's bicycle."

"No, I did not," she insisted. "I just said that if you perhaps paid more attention to who is coming and going, this might not have happened, that's all. Just take more notice while you're sitting here. It's not rocket surgery or anything!"

"I think you meant—oh, forget it. Come on; let's go." Scooter said as he grabbed Traverna Lynn's arm and pulled her away.

I now saw why Arwen did not want Traverna Lynn to take this case by herself. I mouthed "Sorry" to the guard as I shrugged my shoulders and turned

16 6-6 8-6 10-3 2-12 4-2 9-1 13-1 15-9 18-2 2-15 2-2

to join the others. The man growled and then immediately picked his newspaper back up and returned to reading. *Okay, Traverna Lynn might have a point about that guy,* I thought.

With a little more effort than it should have taken, we got Traverna Lynn to calm down and take us to her apartment so we could interview Arwen and check out her bike.

Traverna Lynn told us to wait outside while she went inside to get Arwen. When she came out, she frowned and apologized. "I'm sorry, but I have to warn you: I think Arwen woke up on the wrong side of the room this morning."

"Don't you mean, 'She woke up on the wrong side of the bed'?" AJ asked with a laugh.

"Yeah, that too. I guess she had a fight with some of her Cheer buddies yesterday, so she's a little cranky this morning."

Just then Arwen came out wearing a running outfit and a fake smile. It was pretty clear we had started her day before she had really wanted to, because her hair was mussed up. Of course, she still looked like a red-headed angel.

I tried to say hello, but for once in my life, when I opened up my mouth, no words came out. I just stood there with my jaw hanging open. *Idiot! Say something!* Arwen didn't say hello either, though; it was clear she was not in the mood. She got right down to the business at hand and went around the corner and pulled her bike out of a small closet

6-8 11-5 8-5 20 13-9 18-3 7-8 9-1 5-4 1-13 6-1

attached to the outside patio. Arwen's bicycle was a bright pink mountain bike with splashes of dark blue. After a second look, I realized that the dark blue did not belong on the bike. I figured the blue was actually from Mr. McIntyre's truck and had transferred to Arwen's bike when she had crashed into the truck.

"This is where the brakes snapped," she said as she pointed to a spot above the fork that held the front tire. Scooter bent over to get a closer look. After a moment he stood back up.

"Yeah, it almost looks like it melted. Some sort of acid corroded the metal wire and weakened it. Then one day it just snapped," he said.

"Did you maybe spill something on it?" AJ asked Arwen.

"Something that eats away at metal? Not likely, Aidge," I said, defending her.

"No!" Arwen snapped, her hands on her hips. "Besides, the same thing happened to another girl who I don't even know—if they both happened from spills, that would be a crazy coincidence!"

"I know this sort of looks like an accident, but I don't think that's enough evidence," Traverna Lynn chimed in. "Remember, you can't read a book by its cover."

Arwen rolled her eyes. "You mean, 'Don't *judge* a book by its cover.'" She turned to the three of us. "Please excuse her. She does this all the time, mixes up phrases and stuff."

7-12 3-4 10-4 6-4 14-3 15-1 5-11 22 14-9 7-4 9-1 2-6

"Yeah, we noticed," all three of us said, laughing.

"We will know a lot more after talking to this other girl, Brooklyn. So we had better get to investigating," Scooter said as he dismissed himself.

Arwen's jaw dropped. She appeared shocked that Scooter would just walk away before she was done with him. "Why don't you start by solving *my* bike problem!" she huffed. Scooter kept walking.

"Is there anything else I can do for you, Arwen?" I asked.

AJ slapped me on the back of the head and pulled me away before I could see her response.

"Ouch! What was that for?" I asked hysterically as he pulled me along.

"Because you asked for it!" AJ said, speeding up to catch up to Scooter and Traverna Lynn. I turned back for one more glance at Arwen. She was staring at her bike and shaking her head. *I'm going to make that girl smile again*, I told myself.

Brooklyn was sitting on her front steps, tying her shoes, when we walked up.

"Brooklyn?" Scooter asked as he stretched out his hand.

The girl hesitantly shook his hand and said, "Yeah. Who are you?"

"My name is Scooter. This is Tyler and AJ, and we are the Enigma Squad. We are a detective agency looking into a couple of broken bicycles like yours. Oh, and this is Traverna Lynn. She is a friend. Her sister has a bike that was also broken this week." Traverna Lynn nodded and smiled in satisfaction, happy to be mentioned.

"We were wondering if we could take a look at your bike and see what's wrong with it," I said.

"Um, sure, I guess," she said, getting up. "Let me go get the key to the storage closet." She came out a second later and headed to the side of the apartment with the covered patio. Just like Arwen, she kept her bike in a closet outside, since none of the apartments had garages to store outdoorsy stuff.

Brooklyn's bike was a tangerine mountain bike very similar to Arwen's, and it looked to be just as new, except that this bike did not appear to have a scratch on it.

"So what happened?" AJ jumped in.

"Well, Sunday I was coasting down Silverdale Way, y'know? I started to slow down to turn into this apartment complex, and then I heard the brakes snap. Not much I could do. Lucky I was on a straight road, y'know? Just kept coasting on down the hill till the road got less steep near Silverdale. Then I drug my shoes on the ground till I stopped. My shoes were practically on fire! Then, y'know, I had to pedal all the way back up the hill to get home. That was a bummer!"

Scooter had stopped listening. He was squinting and looking over every inch of the brake cable. He popped up, "Aha, here it is!" He pointed to a spot just below where the cable attached to the handlebars.

8-6 2-1 15-7 17-2 10-1 9-2 17-3 17-4 9-5 3-1 8-4 13-7

"It looks very similar to Arwen's bike. It looks like acid sort of chewed up the cable right here. Except it looks like a lot more acid and less pressure on the brakes made this snap. Brooklyn, how often would you say you rode your bike in the last week?"

"Actually, I been staying at my Grandma's house in Lake Chelan most of the week. The first time I rode was Sunday, when it broke."

"So where did you go Sunday?" Scooter asked.

"I rode down to the clubhouse, to go swimming, y'know? And then I came home to eat lunch, then went up the hill to my friend's house in Spirit Ridge. Then coming back here, the brakes busted, like I told you."

"Hmm. You guys thinking what I am thinking?" Scooter asked.

AJ was eager to answer: "Yeah. Both bikes were at the clubhouse before they were busted!"

"Exactly. And I think that is where we need to go next. Thanks, Brooklyn, for your time. We are going to figure this out." Scooter started to walk off. You could see Scooter was already on a different train of thought, and he was oblivious to anything else going on around him.

"Let us know if you think of anything else that might help our investigation," I told Brooklyn. "And sorry about your bike." Then AJ, Traverna Lynn, and I rushed off to join Scooter.

12-6 16-1 18-9 4-16 2-10 6-1 15-3 10-1 3-3 15-4 7

CHAPTER 5

An Impressive Display

When we caught up to Scooter, he threw out an idea for what we should do next. Since no one had any objections, we decided to put it into action. We had left our bikes over near Traverna Lynn's apartment, so we went and picked them up and rode over to the front of the clubhouse. We left our bikes parked out front and then went inside. When we entered the clubhouse we could see the rental office to our left and a small room to our right that held a big-screen TV. Traverna Lynn said that room was used to host parties. As we continued down the hall, we came to the main attraction of the clubhouse: the swimming pool and hot tub. We went into the room with the pool and then quickly exited through the back door. Scooter wanted anyone who was watching to think we were still inside the clubhouse. We then circled back around and weaved our way among the parked cars until we had made it back to the front steps of the McIntyres' apartment.

"Now we wait," Scooter said as he sat down. "From here we can watch our bikes sitting in front of the clubhouse and see if anyone tampers with them."

This turned out to be one of Scooter's most boring ideas ever. We sat on the front steps of Traverna Lynn's apartment for the next three hours, trying to look casual while at the same time keeping an eye on the clubhouse. Nothing. At least Traverna Lynn was nice enough to go inside and bring us out some lunch. Popsicles and peanut-butter crackers is not exactly what I would have chosen for lunch, but it worked. I was really hoping that Arwen would poke her head out the front door and say hello to me, but it seemed our relationship was going about as well as the stakeout.

"I guess our bikes will not suffer the same fate as the others," Scooter said finally, calling it quits. Barely had those words come out of his mouth, when a group of kids appeared at the entrance to the apartment complex and started walking toward the clubhouse. As they got closer, we could see that one of them had a basketball. They appeared to be coming or going from a pickup basketball game.

"Those could be the same guys Arwen saw the other day," AJ whispered. He didn't have to whisper, though—the basketball group was well outside of hearing range.

"Could be the same guys. Let's watch and see," Scooter said.

The boys neared the clubhouse, but when they reached the entrance where the bikes were parked, they just kept on walking. In fact, they were so caught up in their conversations that not a single boy even turned and looked in that direction. The boys kept walking down the middle of the road and started heading down the hill toward us. They eventually walked right past us on their way to the basketball court, which was just down the street from where we were sitting.

"Well, I think we can cross them off our suspect list," I said.

"Actually, they were never really on the list," Scooter corrected me.

"Waddaya mean?" I asked. "How can you say they were never on the list?"

"Let's go with what we know," Scooter answered. *Grrrr. I hate it when he says that.* He continued, "All we know is that some basketball players happened to be in the vicinity when Arwen discovered her bicycle was broken. We don't even know if that is when the bike was tampered with. It could have happened days—even weeks—earlier, and the bike finally broke just the other day. That acid or whatever it was probably needed some time to eat through the cable. We can't be sure this is the same group of basketball guys, anyway. Besides, these guys don't exactly look like they are capable of handling that stuff."

Oh boy. Scooter would soon learn right alongside the rest of us that you would be surprised what some people are capable of.

AJ stood up. "Okay, since they're not on the list… It looks like they got nine guys over there, so I'm gonna see if I can jump in and play. Enjoy the look-out duty!" He jogged over to the basketball court. A couple kids on skateboards had joined the group when they got to the court, so with the addition of AJ, they had a nice turnout for a pickup game.

I looked over at the clubhouse. Nothing. I looked back at the basketball court. AJ was running around like everyone else. AJ is one of the taller kids in our junior high, but a couple of the basketball players he was playing with today were taller and stronger than him. I figured they must be in high school. Even so, AJ seemed to be hanging in there just fine.

I glanced back over to the clubhouse. Still nothing. I then glanced over at the tall evergreen trees that towered above the fence that surrounded the Birdcage. *What would happen if one of those trees fell,* I wondered. *It would turn the fence into a pile of tooth-picks. But how many sections of the fence would it take out? Five or six? Maybe even more if the tree fell sort of sideways.* I then looked at the clubhouse. I wondered if any of those trees were tall enough that if it fell, it could reach the clubhouse. *Maybe even crush my bike sitting out front? The bikes! Ugh! This is too boring. Nothing is going to happen.* I turned my attention back to the basketball game in progress.

"Okay, I am ready to get out of here. How close

1-2 10-1 18-4 9-9 4-9 6-1 12-7 14-6 2-1 11-8 3-7 9

do you think AJ is to being done over there? What do you think the score is?"

"17–14," Traverna Lynn said matter-of-factly.

"That is a pretty specific guess," Scooter laughed.

"That wasn't a guess. That *is* the score," she insisted.

"How could you know that, sitting way over here?" I asked.

"Because I've been watching," she answered with a smile.

"But there is no scoreboard!" I argued.

"I don't need one. AJ's team has scored eight baskets, and the other team, seven. So then I just had to figure out if they were playing one point for any basket or two points per basket with three pointers for long-distance shots. Well, see that kid in the red shorts on AJ's team? All he does is shoot from the outside, and he always looks down before he shoots. That's because he is making sure he's behind the three-point line painted on the court."

"Wow. I am impressed, Traverna Lynn! You sound like you could be Scooter's long-lost twin."

"Her logic is sound, but we have to see if she's right before you start getting carried away, Ty!" Scooter smirked. He tried to hide it, but I think he was actually impressed with Traverna Lynn's observations.

"Well, if they are playing to 21, then two more baskets by AJ's team should end the game," I announced.

It didn't take long to confirm Traverna Lynn's

17-10 7-2 13-4 1-8 9-4 11-5 4-8 21-2 2-5 15-3 5-2

theory. AJ made the first basket, and as the other team attempted to score, Red-shorts stole the ball and passed it to a wide-open teammate for another easy score. AJ's team exchanged high fives while the other team waited eagerly for a rematch.

Scooter stood up and started heading for the court. "Okay, now I am impressed," he said with a grin.

When we got to the court, Scooter told AJ that we were done watching our bikes *not* get tampered with, and we were ready to do something a little more exciting. AJ was really enjoying the basketball but reluctantly decided to bow out of the next game. One of the skateboarding kids decided to call it quits as well in order to keep the teams even at four on four.

The skateboarder jumped on his board and immediately fell off and did a faceplant in the beauty bark near the basketball court. All the ball players laughed insensitively while the skateboarder picked up his board and began inspecting it.

"Shoot, my front truck just snapped! Now I'm gonna have to head to the shop and get it replaced!"

Traverna Lynn leaned over to me and joked, "Hey, maybe our bike vandal is leafing out and messing with skateboards too!"

"The expression is 'branching out,'" I corrected her with a laugh.

"Whatever!" She threw her hands up and laughed as she walked away toward the clubhouse.

6 4-3 8-3 10-2 1-5 5-5 3-1 3-4 7-2 13-6 4-3 11-4 6

I started to follow but noticed that Scooter was not coming. He was staring off into space with that look on his face. I call it his "thinking face." Whenever he is onto something, he makes this half-smile, half-frown expression with his mouth. That face can't be duplicated, and neither can his ideas that come from it. He broke out of his trance and started walking toward me. By this time AJ had joined us as well.

"Something that kid said has got me thinking," Scooter said as we went to get our bikes from the clubhouse. "The police might not have had any bike crimes reported lately, but I know one place that would know if more bikes have been broken lately."

I could see where he was going with this train of thought. "A bicycle repair shop!" I interrupted.

"Exactly! And the only one around is Ye Olde Cycle Shoppe in Old-Town Silverdale. Anyone up for another ride into town?"

"How about we just call them?" I whined. The town of Silverdale had started down by the waterfront and had slowly expanded north, toward where we lived, over the years. The older portions of town down by the water were still referred to as Old-Town Silverdale. If we wanted to visit the bike shop, we were going to have to ride to the far side of town to get there. No thanks!

We had caught up to Traverna Lynn, and she chimed in, "Actually, if we head down there, then we can take Arwen's bike to get fixed!"

Scooter and AJ readily agreed, and I realized this

19-11 12-5 5-2 4-2 2-3 7-1 8-4 11-5 17-9 18-3 15-4 10-1

might be my chance to impress Arwen by getting her bike fixed for her. It was clear her bike meant a lot to her, and if she thought I was the one who helped get it fixed, then that might score me a few points with her.

Traverna Lynn went into her house and came back a short time later, wearing a camouflage back-pack that matched her shoes. Sticking out of the top of it was her skateboard. "In case they need to keep the bike overnight, I have a ride back," she said. She then went over to the covered patio, grabbed Arwen's bike, and hopped on. Traverna Lynn is much smaller than Arwen, so getting on the bike was quite a feat. When she sat on the seat, her feet dangled on each side but didn't touch the ground. She had to lean the bike quite a bit to the side in order to rest one foot on the ground. Pretty entertaining to watch, if you ask me.

So after a pretty good laugh at Traverna Lynn's bike antics, we headed out, starting the trek down the hill and then to the other side of town. The first part of the ride became a little scary when we remembered that Traverna Lynn had no brakes. But we didn't think about that fact until it was too late. Luckily, we hit the first intersection when the light was green and then the rest of the trip was pretty level, so she didn't have any problems. When we finally got to the bike shop, it was almost 3:30. That meant we didn't have a lot of time to talk before I needed to start the trip home in order to get there by

13-2 24 7-5 11-4 15-3 21-6 15-6 8-3 3-1 18-2

dinner. I was not about to earn one of Mom's classic lectures on punctuality.

2-3 1-12 2-18 2-8 1-16 2-10 14

CHAPTER 6
Beyond the Birdcage

As we entered Ye Olde Cycle Shoppe, I noticed hanging in the front window a couple mountain bikes very similar to Arwen's, which Traverna Lynn had wheeled into the store with us. It was probably a good bet that this was where her bike had come from.

Even with huge windows letting in lots of daylight, it still took a few seconds for our eyes to adjust to the indoors after being out in the bright sunlight.

"Just a sec!" A voice came from somewhere behind the counter. As my eyes continued to adjust, I realized there was a doorway behind the counter, and through the doorway there appeared to be various tools hanging on a wall. I moved a little to my left, and I could see that there were also lots of shelves with rows upon rows of small boxes. I figured that must be the stock room where they kept tools and spare parts.

After what was clearly longer than "a sec," a tall kid with badly dyed black hair walked out of the stock room and placed his greasy hands on the counter. Both his hands and arms were spotted with grease, and his left forearm had a scary-looking tattoo that spelled "E-Free" in black letters. His T-shirt promoted the name of a band I had never listened to, and judging by the artwork on the T-shirt, my parents would make sure it stayed that way. I guessed by the grease on his T-shirt and arms that "E-Free" must be the guy who does all the dirty work of fixing stuff. He pulled his arms back from the counter, and then I realized that I had been staring at his tattoo and he had caught me.

"Can I help you?" he asked, sounding uninterested in actually helping us. It was clear this guy was hired for his mechanical skills and not his customer service.

"Yes. My sister bought this bike here. I am wondering if you can fix the brakes?" Traverna Lynn asked.

"Sure," he said, coming around the counter. He ran his hand along the brake cable until he reached the damaged part of the line. "It will be nineteen dollars for a new cable and fifteen for an hour of labor to replace it."

"But she just bought it three weeks ago! Isn't there a warranty or something?" Traverna Lynn asked.

"Doesn't matter. See this?" He held the damaged portion of the brake line in his hand. "This isn't a

9-4 7-1 12-10 15-1 2-6 8-1 16-10 13-4 13-5 2-2 4-4 2-5

defect in the bike. This looks like somebody messed with this bike."

Scooter jumped in, "That is sort of what we thought it looked like too. Do you know what might have been used to cause this sort of damage?"

"No clue. Sorry," he said, letting go of the brake cable and walking back behind the counter. "So you wanna pay to get it fixed or what?"

Scooter jumped in again before Traverna Lynn could answer him. "So uh, do you work here often?"

"E-Free" looked confused by such a random question. "Uh, yeah, during the summer it's just me stuck in here all by myself until the boss comes in around three. Today he's late because he had to go down to Tacoma to pick up some extra parts. Which reminds me, I gotta run; I'm already behind on repairs he thinks I should have done."

Scooter continued with his questioning. "So you are behind on repairs? Would you say that the number of repairs you have done in recent weeks has been higher than normal?"

"Not at all. It's summer, and bikes get more use when school's out. It's perfectly normal for us to be swamped this time of year." He began to get frustrated. "Look, I gotta get back to work. Do you want the bike fixed or not?"

Just then, some commotion came from the back room, followed by a man hollering, "Eddie, get back here and help me bring in these boxes!"

"Shoot! My boss just got back! See? Now I am

3-1 13-2 18-4 3-8 14-3 6-9 10-5 7-2 1-8 17-7 8-4 6-11

in trouble because you guys kept me out here yakking!" "E-Free," whose real name was apparently Eddie, whispered to us. "Coming," he shouted to the boss in the other room.

He ripped a pink message note off the pad sitting next to the cash register and handed it to Traverna Lynn. "If you want me to fix the bike, leave it here and leave your phone number on the paper. I'll call you when I can get to it." With that said, he disappeared into the back room before any of us could respond. Traverna Lynn quickly wrote her info down, and we hustled out of the store.

Since Traverna Lynn was on a skateboard, we let her get a head start on the way home while the three of us talked for a minute. "Well, they did *not* hire 'E-Free' for his people skills," I joked as we watched Traverna Lynn skating away.

"Ain't that the truth!" AJ agreed.

"I don't know that we really learned much here," Scooter said as we got on our bikes. "But I just got an idea of what to do next."

"And that is?" AJ asked.

"We can talk about it after dinner," Scooter replied with a wink and then rode off smiling. AJ and I chased after him, hoping he would explain further. I was not holding my breath, though. Scooter got some kind of sick joy by keeping us in the dark at times, and this looked like it was going to be one of those times.

The rest of the ride home was uneventful. We

passed up Traverna Lynn in no time and had to stop often to wait for her to catch up. We eventually made it to the Birdcage, where we said goodbye to her. Then we slowly pedaled the rest of the way up the hill to Westridge. Scooter suggested we meet down in HQ after dinner, and out of sheer curiosity, AJ and I agreed.

Dinner at my house was pretty boring except for the fact that Mom said she talked to Dad for a minute, and he said he would be coming home two weeks earlier than planned. That meant he would be home by the following Friday! That was very good news indeed! It had only been a month and a half since the Navy sent my dad's boat out to sea, but it seemed like it had been forever since I last saw him.

Still thinking about the great news about Dad, I didn't even notice the trip over to Scooter's house or down the ladder to HQ. When I got inside HQ, Scooter was typing away at his computer. AJ wasn't there yet.

"So what's up, Scoot? What's your big plan?" I asked. I wasn't going to wait for AJ to show up. He was probably still eating dinner; AJ was not one to leave a meal early.

"Hm? Oh, right. Well, I figured that Arwen's and Brooklyn's bikes couldn't be the only ones tampered with, but so far in our investigation, that seems to be the case. The police haven't heard of anything; the bike shop hasn't heard of anything. So I thought we would try one more thing before I decide that I was wrong."

AJ arrived toward the end of that and jumped right into the conversation, "Wrong about what?"

"Ever hear of the two-minute rule?" Scooter asked, annoyed by the interruption.

"No, what is it?" AJ asked. "Is it like the two-minute warning in football?"

"No," said Scooter, "it has to do with listening for two minutes before joining a conversation." He turned away from AJ and continued with his story. "So as you know, we now have a website, EnigmaSquad.com, where people can get in contact with us if they want to hire us."

"Yeah, we know about that already," I said, pushing Scooter to get to the point.

"So when I set up our website, I also created a place where people could sign up to help us if we ever needed it. I asked them to join 'The Network.' I have over twenty kids from school signed up for The Network. I say we start using them now."

Scooter then went on to explain that he was sending an email to each member of The Network asking them to do three things: first, report to EnigmaSquad.com if they had heard of any bicycle or skateboard or scooter or any other wheeled vehicle that had been damaged in any way—preferably in the last couple weeks; second, try and get an exact address of where the bike or whatever was damaged; and lastly, forward an identical message to ten

6-13 11-2 16-4 10-4 25 6-3 19-1 21-4 6-13 18-2 3-1 8-7

more people who were not yet in The Network.

"So if everyone in The Network passes the message on to ten more people, we could have over two hundred people being our eyes and ears for us!" Scooter said.

"Now we can sit back and let The Network work for us!" AJ said as he walked over to the fridge and unconsciously looked to see what was inside.

Really, AJ? I thought. *Didn't you just eat?*

"If a bike is broken anywhere near here, we are going to know about it pretty soon," Scooter said.

I didn't have very high hopes for Scooter's Network idea. After all, most teenagers aren't that observant. Not like us, anyway. It was still pretty early in the evening, but we were all pretty worn out from the day's adventures. So AJ and I just played some chess while Scooter fiddled around on his computer. The great thing about playing chess without Scooter is that someone besides Scooter is guaranteed to win!

It didn't take long to prove just how wrong I was about Scooter's idea. We had only been playing for about fifteen minutes when he spoke up to say he had already received a response from The Network.

"You know Miles Seaborn, who rides our bus?" he asked.

"Who?" AJ asked.

"You know: the tall kid who sits in the back of the bus, always talking about basketball and disc golf?"

8-3 15-2 7-1 17-2 5-4 18-11 23 7-6 17-1 4-5 12-1 15-4

"Oh yeah," AJ said. "I know who you're talking about now. He was too busy playing for some all-star team, so he didn't play basketball for our junior high this past year."

"Yeah? Well, anyway, he just reported that recently his next door neighbor up in Spirit Ridge discovered a bent front wheel on his ten-speed bike." Scooter turned back to his computer, "Oh, here is another one. Does anyone know where Hidden Place is? Apparently a little boy's dirt bike had the handle-bars break while he was riding on that road."

"No, I don't know where that is," I said. "Why don't you look up the address on a map? Just pull it up on the computer."

"I have a better idea," Scooter said as he stood up and headed for the door. "Stay here; I will be right back."

He disappeared out the vault door and came back in no time at all. He was carrying some tape and one of those foldout maps that you might carry in the glove compartment of your car. When fold-ed up, the map was smaller than a notebook, but Scooter began to unfold it and lay it out across the small round table we had in HQ. The map, show-ing *Silverdale, WA, and Surrounding Cities,* was almost five feet across and nearly three feet tall. It was way bigger than the tabletop. I don't know how anyone ever expects you to be able to look at a map like that while seated in a car, or more importantly how they expect you to fold it back up when you're done!

"I was thinking we could tape this whole thing to the wall and then mark where the Network reports bike problems and see if we notice any sort of pattern," Scooter said.

AJ grabbed one corner of the map, and I grabbed another. We stretched it out against the wall so Scooter could tape it there. But Scooter had a hard time taping the map to the wall. The concrete walls were sort of bumpy, and the tape really needed a smooth surface to work properly. Finally, he got the tape to stick, and then he started to put red Xs on the map where the two tips from the Network were located. As he began to write, the tape released itself from the wall, and the map came crashing down. Scooter let out a frustrated sigh and then plopped down on the couch to think.

"We could always just use the table," AJ suggested.

Scooter dismissed the idea with a wave of his hand. Scooter sat on the couch in "thinking mode" while AJ and I patiently watched him. Almost on cue, Scooter jumped up, presumably with an idea, ready to put it into action.

"I guess it's time to decorate," he said as he moved toward the door. "You guys move the couch and stuff away from that wall, and I will be right back."

"Huh?" AJ and I said in near unison. But Scooter was already gone.

This time when Scooter left, it seemed to take a lot longer for him to make it back. When he finally did, he was carrying a pail of paint, a couple

11-11 12-3 2-6 2-7 4-2 9-15 30 5-1 8-9 13-7

paintbrushes, and a couple face masks. Scooter was already wearing a mask; he looked like he was getting ready to perform surgery.

Without saying a word, he opened up the paint can and began to paint the wall opposite the fridge and sink. I wasn't sure what his plan was, but I took this as my cue and grabbed the other paintbrush to begin painting on the same wall. AJ just stood there and let out an audible "Wha?" every few minutes. It didn't take long before we had the one wall painted. Scooter immediately began cleaning up. He acted as if he were suddenly in a big hurry.

"If we're going to paint one wall, shouldn't we paint them all?" I asked.

"Nope." Scooter didn't offer any more explanation than that. He hurried over to the sink to wash his hands.

I hate it when Scooter gets like that. He knows exactly what the plan is, but for some reason he gets a kick out of keeping AJ and me in the dark. After washing his hands, Scooter turned around and stared at the wall, admiring our recent work. The wall was now a purple color with a bit of a sparkle to it. It looked pretty cool compared to the dull grey concrete of the other walls.

"Not the color I would have chosen, but it ought to do the trick," Scooter said. He gathered up his things as if he were leaving.

"If it isn't the color you would have chosen, then why'd you just paint the wall that color? And why

10-3 12-4 8-1 5-7 16-2 19-1 6-3 9-7 1-4 14-2 19-6 10-1

only one wall?" AJ persisted.

"Yeah, how did we go from mapping out broken bicycles to painting HQ?" I added.

"I promise to show you both tomorrow," he said, "but right now I just have to get out of here. There is not a lot of ventilation down here, and the smell of paint is really getting to me. I will take care of the rest of the cleanup stuff. Why don't we just meet here tomorrow morning?"

AJ and I had done enough guessing for one day, so we happily agreed to leave Scooter to do whatever it was he was going to do. I still had some time before my curfew, so I went with AJ to his house and ended up getting sucked into an action movie on his big flatscreen TV. I didn't think about Scooter or HQ or bicycles or anything else related to the case for the rest of the night.

8-6 9-8 13-20 5

CHAPTER 7

The Mysterious Gift

The next morning I met up with AJ at his house, and we went over to HQ together. When we got to the metal plate, it was propped open about an inch with a block of wood. A slight breeze with a faint paint smell was pouring out of the opening. I looked at AJ as if to ask why, but he just shrugged his shoulders. *So much for security*, I thought. When we went down the ladder, we could see that the vault door was propped open as well. The smell of paint was stronger down there but still not too bad.

When we walked into HQ we found Scooter drawing a red *X* on the map, which was now spread out on the freshly painted wall. The map appeared to be held in place by Utah, Pennsylvania, and Texas. These were little refrigerator magnets that were normally stuck to the front of the Parks' fridge. *But now they're stuck to the wall?* I wondered.

"Oh good, I am glad you guys are here. I need some help. We got forty replies to our message last night! We have a lot of mapping to do!"

"Whoa-whoa-whoa, back up!" AJ demanded. "You said you were going to fill us in on your crazy actions from yesterday!"

"Right you are. So sorry," Scooter apologized. "Okay, so where to start..."

"How about you start with why out of the blue you decided to paint a wall last night?" I jumped in.

"Oh, yes. Well, as you saw, our map was not going to stay up on the wall very well with the tape we were using. So I was thinking of ways we could get it to stay up, and then I remembered that my mom was painting her sewing room with this paint. The other day, she was explaining to Wyatt that it sparkled because it is metallic paint—there are little flecks of metal in the paint, which give it the sparkle. So I was thinking about our map problem, and I thought it would be nice to hold the map to the wall like refrigerator magnets hold artwork or school announcements to the door of the fridge. So when I left here, I went inside my house, took one of the magnets from the fridge, and went upstairs to my mom's sewing room. Sure enough, it sticks to the wall; the magnet holds to the metal in the paint! So I decided to paint the walls here in HQ so we could do the same thing with the map.

"I did not, however, account for the smell. So I had to get out of here last night before the fumes made me sick. Otherwise I would have painted all the walls. Anyway, last night after you left and I had

2-13 17-7 9-1 15-6 1-4 8-5 4-9 9-5 14-2 16-2 3-12

gotten some fresh air, I came back down here and brought this small fan to try and help the paint dry faster and maybe get rid of some of the smell. So I had to prop the lid to HQ open to help move air faster."

"So much for your super-security measures, huh?" AJ joked.

"It was an acceptable risk," Scooter replied. "I also painted a couple scraps of wood and left them near the edge of the lawn. So if anyone smelled the paint and started wondering where the smell was coming from, they would find the wooden pieces and figure that those were the source of the smell."

"This morning I came down with some magnets, and sure enough, they stuck to the wall like I thought they would! So I put up our map of Silverdale and had just started plotting our results from The Network when you guys showed up."

Satisfied with his explanation, AJ and I jumped right in and helped plot the points on the map that corresponded to the tips that were coming in from The Network. It took us about an hour to check the responses and then figure out where they were on the map. A broken bicycle chain at 447 Schold Road, another snapped brake line over on High Sierra Lane, a flat tire just off Ridgetop Boulevard. It was sort of like a weird scavenger hunt.

When we were done, we took a step back to look at the map and see what it looked like from a bird's-eye view. There were well over thirty red Xs spread all over the map of Silverdale with quite a few Xs clustered within the Birdcage.

"It looks like our bike vandal has been pretty busy!" AJ observed.

"It's true. He or she has," Scooter added, "but we have to remember that some of these reports probably have nothing to do with someone tampering with the bicycle. Some of these red Xs just represent bad luck or simple wear and tear."

"So what do we do know?" AJ asked. "That's a lot of people to try and interview to figure out if each red X was from foul play or an accident."

"Good question. I think all this exercise has confirmed so far is that the problem is bigger than just Arwen's and Brooklyn's bicycles."

Just then we heard a *chirp chirp*. It was the HQ phone, and it was ringing. The phone had a ring that sounded like a bird chirping because a normal ring might be heard outside of HQ, and it might attract unwanted attention. Scooter picked up the phone on the third ring (or chirp).

"Enigma Squad at your service, this is Scooter… Oh hey, Mom!" He listened for a few moments and then finished the phone call with "Okay, we will be right there."

"My mom says she just checked the mail, and I got a package! She thinks it's a book."

"Were you expecting a book?" I asked.

"Not that I know of. So let's go check it out!" he said as he headed for the door. AJ and I followed close behind.

We decided to leave the fan on and the door and lid propped open as they had been overnight so that HQ could air out a little longer. When we walked in the back door, Scooter's package was sitting on the kitchen counter. Mrs. Parks had guessed that inside was a book. That was a pretty safe guess. The package was almost the exact shape of some of the larger library books I had checked out for summer pleasure reading. AJ and I wanted Scooter to rip the package open so we could see what was inside, but Scooter paused.

"Mom, you said this was in the *mailbox* today?" he hollered to Mrs. Parks, who was folding laundry in the other room.

"Yes, Sean. Today. I called you the second I got it."

Scooter lowered his voice. "Hmm, interesting. Check this out, guys: there is no return address, and although it was in my mailbox, it has no postage stamps on it. That means someone actually *placed* this in my mailbox. They did not *send* it."

The hairs on the back of my neck tingled as Scooter cautiously began to open the package. As he unwrapped the plain brown paper, I caught myself holding my breath.

"Oh, wow!" Scooter exclaimed as he revealed what was inside. It was a copy of *The Adventures of Sherlock Holmes*. The cover was made of real leather, and the edges of the pages were lined with gold. It was absolutely beautiful! I don't know a lot about

14-8 17-1 3-6 11-11 7-11 12-4 16-1 1-4 37 8-4 16-6 3-1

the value of books, but I'm guessing it was pretty expensive.

Sticking out of the top of the book was a piece of paper folded in thirds. It looked like it was being used as a makeshift bookmark. Scooter opened the book to the page marked with the piece of paper and then unfolded the piece of paper. He laughed out loud! AJ and I were puzzled until he handed the paper to me.

The piece of paper was actually a photocopy of the article that had run in our school's newspaper— the same article that Arwen had seen—where they had interviewed Scooter after the Enigma Squad had solved *The Case of the Old Man in the Mailbox*. Scooter was laughing because in the article, he had mentioned that his inspiration for solving crimes was Sherlock Holmes. That quote had been highlighted.

"Ooh-la-la, Scoot. It looks like you have a secret admirer!" I joked as I handed the paper back to him.

"Hey, look at the book!" AJ said, pointing at the opened book. "There are numbers written on the bottom of this page."

We all looked down and saw that AJ was right. There were a bunch of numbers at the bottom of the right page but none on the left. Scooter turned the page to find more numbers on the next page, and the next, and the next. He quickly flipped through the entire book to see if the numbers were on any other pages.

"Interesting. It appears that my so-called admirer

5-3 20-13 9-1 4-7 13-4 17-7 1-2 12-5 11-5 14-6 4 5-10 has left me some sort of number code. The numbers are only on the bottom of pages 141 through 144, and apparently they placed this bookmark here so I would see where the code started."

"And you have no clue who could have given this to you?" I asked.

"None at all!"

"Well, your secret admirer knows you pretty well, whoever it is. Sending you a gorgeous copy of one of your favorite books, and leaving you a secret code to figure out too!" I said excitedly.

We turned our attention back to the book and the number code at the bottom of the page. The first line started like this:

23–8 4–15 1–19 4–47 17–17 11–31 3–9

There were just a bunch of number pairs with dashes in between. This code continued along the bottom of the next few pages, and occasionally a few numbers without pairs were mixed in.

"So what do you think it means?" AJ asked. "How do we solve it?"

Scooter frowned. "Hmm. I would have guessed that the numbers stood for letters of the alphabet, but I see a 47 here, and there are only twenty-six letters in the alphabet. I don't think that's it."

"Maybe this is a math puzzle. Those dashes could be minus signs or something," I suggested.

"Could be. We will have to keep that in mind. Let's get on the computer and do some research."

"Sounds good to me," AJ said as he headed for

2-7 9-4 16-3 19-6 3-5 12-5 11-8 8-11 17-4 5-1 2-2 3-3

the door to the backyard. He lowered his voice so Mrs. Parks wouldn't hear, "I was starting to get hungry! And even though this is a kitchen, your mom doesn't exactly keep a lot of snacks lying around."

"Of course you are hungry, AJ. But actually I was thinking we would go upstairs and use the remote computer in my room, so we can stay away from the paint fumes for a little while longer."

Reluctantly, AJ agreed that was probably a better idea than using the computer in HQ, and so we all headed upstairs. The smaller computer Scooter had in his room was really just used to connect with the computer in HQ and all its cool abilities. So we were actually going to be using the supercomputer inside HQ anyway. But that wasn't going to solve any of AJ's hunger problems.

Scooter felt like he already spent way too much time on the computer as it was, so he said when it came to researching stuff on the internet, that was my job. So Scooter typed in a couple commands to connect me to his supercomputer down in HQ and then let me have the seat at the computer desk. I clicked on the internet icon, and Scooter's homepage automatically came up, the online version of the local newspaper. Scooter liked to keep up with local news; he liked to think we might find our next case that way. I clicked over to a search engine and typed in "number code" as a start to our research.

"Wait, wait—go back," Scooter demanded.

14 3-4 5-1 1-33 7-6 9-4 10-3 14-2 15-12 7-8 14

"Go back where? I haven't even searched any-thing yet."

"Go back to my homepage. I think I saw something."

I clicked the *Back* arrow until we were back at the online newspaper page. We all stared at the page for about half a minute until AJ couldn't stand the silence anymore. "Okay, guys, what am I missing?"

"Silver-Days are starting tomorrow," Scooter said.

"So what?" AJ countered. "They have Silver-Days every year right after school gets out. That's not exactly news."

"Yes, but look here. This year they are kicking things off with a 5K Fun Run and then a cross-coun-try mountain-bike race. Are you guys thinking what I am thinking?" Scooter asked excitedly.

"That's a lot of bicycles that will all be in the same spot!" I said. I was pretty sure I knew where Scooter's thoughts were headed.

"Exactly! If our vandal knows about this race, he—or she—won't be able to resist being there!"

Since the race was less than a day away, we knew we didn't have a lot of time to prepare. Scooter's new book and the code inside seemed far less important as we began to plan out how we could use the Silver-Days bike race to catch the bike vandal in the act. AJ said he would enter the race in order to have the closest view possible, but I knew that was not the reason at all. AJ just loves competition, and it would be miserable for him to be there watching a race

8-11 16-1 8-6 11-8 14-2 5-3 10-2 2-4 3-1

that he wasn't actually competing in. We decided to bring in Traverna Lynn for our plan and give her the boring but important job of keeping a lookout at the staging area, where the competitors would keep their bikes before and after the race. That seemed the most likely place for the bike-breaking to take place. Scooter and I would mingle and keep our eyes open for any suspicious people throughout the day. And naturally, we would watch our friend AJ compete in the race.

Scooter called Traverna Lynn to tell her of the plan, and of course she was delighted to help in any way that involved her being a part of the team. We then spent the rest of the day over at AJ's house. He had just entered a bike race at the last minute, and so he was very unprepared. We had to fix his helmet to fit the way it was supposed to, find clothes to wear for the competition, and take care of the hardest part—getting his bike into racing condition. One finely tuned bicycle and three greasy boys later, it was about time for dinner, and all three of us just wanted to eat and then fast-forward to the excitement that was coming the next day.

32 5-6 2-2 15-2 9-3 13-3 7-2 3-5 8-4 4-7 32

CHAPTER 8
On Your Mark, Get Set, Go!

The next day the three of us boys met at my house at 7 a.m., and then we headed down the hill to pick up Traverna Lynn. Scooter carried a big backpack that he said was full of some video equipment, so we could perhaps catch a crime on film. AJ carried a backpack with an extra shirt, shoes, and socks (and a whole bunch of snacks). And me? I normally would carry a backpack with every possible thing I could ever possibly need in it, but today I decided to travel light. So all I had with me was a water bottle, which attached to my bike, and some cash, which I had shoved inside my sock because my soccer shorts didn't have any pockets. It was supposed to be lunch money, but I was probably going to buy some ice cream instead. We rode down the hill at supersonic speed and turned into the Birdcage.

Traverna Lynn had decided to ride her bike instead of skateboarding, so it was no time at all before we were in Old-Town Silverdale, where AJ was supposed to check in. We could see it was super crowded with all the people attending the festival, so three of us ditched our bikes and locked them to a telephone pole outside the Old-Town Silverdale Feed Store. AJ had to keep his bike and have it inspected when he checked in for the race. It was only 9 a.m., but as we weaved our way through the crowds toward the race check-in, I could smell the funnel cakes being cooked somewhere nearby; at that moment I knew what I was spending my lunch money on.

After AJ checked in and had his bike inspected, they took it and placed it directly behind the check-in tables. The bicycle staging area behind the tables was a large square with three wooden roadblocks lining each side, the kind that police use when they direct traffic before and after big sporting events. *Yep, if I were trying to damage some bikes today, this is where I would strike*, I said to myself.

It was now 9:30, and the race started at 11. AJ excused himself to go stretch and "clear his mind" before the race. I joked that the "clearing his mind" part would take about ten seconds, so that would leave plenty of time for stretching.

That left Scooter, Traverna Lynn, and me to be on the lookout for the next hour and a half. Since the check-in was so close to the water, we found that if we went and sat on the edge of Silverdale's one big pier with our feet hanging over the water, we had a great view of the roadblock square full of bikes.

Traverna Lynn and I sat down and talked while Scooter set up a camera to record anything suspicious that might happen near the corralled bicycles. Traverna Lynn agreed to stay seated there on the pier until the racers came to get their bicycles for the race. Scooter set the video camera next to her and pressed record. As long as she didn't bump it, the camera would capture everything for the next couple hours. And if she didn't make it obvious by staring directly at someone, they would probably walk by and not even notice her or the camera.

Scooter turned from the camera and asked, "So, Traverna Lynn, are you sure that you'll be okay sitting here for a while? You won't get too bored?"

"Hey, if worse comes to shove, at least I'll get a good suntan!" she joked.

Scooter and I headed off to find AJ. It took us forever to find him, though, so by the time we did, the race was getting ready to start. There was no time to relieve Traverna Lynn from lookout duty. Hopefully, she wouldn't be upset and think we forgot about her.

"Sorry, Traverna Lynn!" I said aloud. Not that she could hear me, but I thought it might make me feel less guilty.

Although they had several different divisions based on age, gender, and skill level, all the racers started the race at the same time. Out of the two-hundred-plus racers at the starting line, AJ had said that there were only a handful of kids he was competing against.

9-11 7-1 8-6 17-1 12-5 2-6 5-4 3-1 8-2 14-2 64

So the race course started by going up Newberry Hill, a very steep road. At the top the racers would turn off the road into the woods, where there were some mountain-biking trails that most of them would be familiar with. After about three miles of trails in the woods, the racers would then pop back out of the woods at about the same place they went in. Then they would rush back down the hill into town and cross the finish line. The festival had set up a huge TV screen near the start/finish line, and they had cameramen placed throughout the woods so that everyone could watch the race without leaving the heart of the festival.

Scooter and I were going to watch the big screen with rapt attention because we knew the woods portion of the race was all that really mattered. If AJ were ahead of the other teenagers by the time he hit the downhill portion of the race, then he had it made. Newberry Hill was way too steep for anyone to pass anyone else—especially to pass AJ.

As the riders were getting set and ready to go, I looked around to see if I knew any other teenagers who might be competing against AJ. Right next to AJ was our friend James Killroy. He was AJ's teammate on the junior-high basketball team. Good guy. There were a couple other kids that looked smaller and younger than AJ, but I was pretty sure that AJ would be able to beat them. I tried to look deeper into the mass of people and bicycles, and that's when I spotted him: Rick Rain. Ugh, I couldn't stand that

6-3 8-2 17-9 4-3 10-3 15-3 15-8 18-1 4-4 9-3

guy. Rick Rain was a kid who lived just down the street from us in the Westridge neighborhood. He had fiery red hair and freckles over every inch of his arms and face. He rode our bus during the school year, and he must have thought his job was to make the trip to school as uncomfortable as possible for AJ, Scooter, and me. He would get onto the bus at the stop before ours, and he would sit in the front seat. Then after we got on at our stop, he would get up and move to whichever seat was directly behind one of us. He would stick his knees into the back of our seat or put nasty stuff in our hair. Luckily, he had been in ninth grade last year, which meant that when summer was over, he would be in tenth grade at the high school and out of our hair and our lives for a long time. I suddenly had a panicked thought. What if Rick didn't pass ninth grade? He wasn't the smartest kid on the block, so that was quite a possibility. Scooter groaned when I told him about seeing Rick.

Just then, the gun went off to start the race, and the riders took off. I would have to save my worries about Rick Rain for a later time. Scooter and I waited in silence for riders to appear on the big screen, which would mean that they had finished climbing the hill and had entered the woods. After a few boring minutes, the first group of the riders appeared on the screen. Most of them were older and more experienced riders. At least that was what I assumed, based on their fancy racing uniforms and their

4-4 15-2 2-5 12-3 17-9 13-1 19-2 18

mountainous leg muscles. Many more adults and a few minutes went by before I saw the first teenager come across the screen. It was AJ's teammate, James. Not far behind him was AJ, followed by Rick. The big screen kept switching to different views of the race in the woods. Every once in a while, Rick or AJ or James would appear in a camera angle, but it was hard to tell who was in the lead. Pretty soon we could see some of the riders coasting around the bend and flying down the long stretch toward the finish line, so we stopped watching the screen and started watching for AJ, Rick, or James to come speeding around the corner.

We weren't disappointed. AJ appeared first around the corner. I jumped and gave a shout: "Woohoo!" Then right behind him came Rick, pedaling feverishly to catch up! AJ was coasting down the hill like lightning, obviously not thinking about anyone behind him. But I could see Rick, a couple feet behind AJ, closing in fast! Two hundred yards from the finish, Rick made his move. He tried to pass AJ. Suddenly, his front tire bumped AJ's back tire! They both swerved and crashed into the tall roadside grass. I heard gasps all around me. Both boys jumped up and scrambled to their bikes. But while they were getting back on, James went flying past them and coasted to an easy win for the teenage division. AJ managed to stay ahead of Rick for the last stretch and came in second. Rick came in third.

6-6 15-1 19-2 12-2 1-9 5-1 11-4 9-4 12-7 5-6 14-4 8-2

Scooter and I ran over to see if AJ was okay; it had looked like a nasty crash. He said he was perfectly fine and was grateful for the soft landing in the grass. Yes, he should be glad it was not on the pavement! Crazy Rick didn't even come over and apologize for making him crash. It didn't really matter, though; AJ knew he would have won, and that's what matters. And if he couldn't, at least it was our friend James who got the win. Plus, we later learned that first, second, and third all got the same prize: a T-shirt with a bunch of silver stick-figures dancing on the front.

After getting AJ's prize and checking on the condition of his bicycle, which was in pretty good shape, we went over to check on Traverna Lynn and see if she had any news for us.

Traverna Lynn said that a few people had stopped by to admire the bikes in the staging area, but no one had touched the bikes as far as she could tell. Even if she had missed anything—which I doubted that she had—Scooter had video footage as a backup.

"Scooter and I didn't see anything or hear anyone complaining about their bike breaking down, so I guess we struck out too," I told her.

"It appears our bike vandal did not feel today was as perfect an opportunity as we did," Scooter added. "But the morning wasn't a complete waste. We got to see a pretty exciting finish to AJ's race."

"It was, huh?" Traverna Lynn said.

"I'm really sorry you missed it," I apologized,

6-6 10-7 15-3 3-3 9-3 3-2 15-1 18-3 4-10 12-7 1-2 8-2

feeling guilty that we had left her there to be bored.

"Hey, no sweat! The next broken bike could be anywhere. We had to spread out; it would be stupid for us to put all our chickens in the same basket," she answered.

"Uh, yeah, exactly," I said as I rolled my eyes and laughed.

1-5 12 5-6 2-5 4-8 7-5 6-14 3-6 5-1 4-10 2-2 4-3

CHAPTER 9
Pizza Epiphany

We left the waterfront and wandered around the various booths for about an hour before we finally went to go pick up our bikes. On the walk to the Feed Store, where we had stashed the bikes, AJ whined that he was starving.

Traverna Lynn hesitantly spoke up. "Do you all like pizza? I know of a place that's pretty good, and it's sort of on the way home. I think it's called Seabeck Pizza."

"Oh my goodness, I love Seabeck Pizza!" I said. I jumped on her suggestion and pretty much ended the discussion right then and there: "Seabeck Pizza, it is!"

Seabeck Pizza has a thicker crust than two of my fingers pressed together. Combine that golden crust with heaps of melted cheese and some spicy pepperoni, and you have the best pizza in town! Just the thought of it was enough for me to forget that I had not gotten any funnel cake. After walking and riding a bike for most of the morning, I was sure that pizza would hit the spot perfectly. I would not be disappointed.

A short bike ride later, we were sitting at a table, waiting for greatness. As the four of us waited for our pizza to be cooked, our conversation turned to the broken bikes.

"So since today was sort of a bust, does that mean we're back to the square drawing board?" Traverna Lynn asked.

AJ laughed.

Scooter answered, "I think we will just have to wait and see where this vandal strikes next. I have The Network working on it."

"The Network?" Traverna Lynn asked.

"Yes," he said. "We have a bunch of kids from our school who are on the lookout for us. If they see or hear of any bikes getting tampered with, they will let us know."

"Oh, cool."

"Yeah," I said, "we already have a bunch of leads to follow up on. But a lot of those bikes were broken before your sister's, so the clues are going to be cold."

Scooter added, "Exactly. So I think we may have to wait for another crime to happen for the trail to heat up again."

Just then, our pizza arrived. Piping-hot, thick-crust pizza: it really doesn't get any better than that. As we started to serve ourselves, the manager came over to our table carrying a big book. He had gray hair and was hunched over even when he wasn't leaning over our table. He set the big book down in between Scooter and AJ.

"I need to borrow your young eyes for a second," he said. "My delivery driver is lost, and I need to give him some directions. Flip to the back, and see if you can find Mockingbird Lane in the index."

Scooter fumbled with the pages until he found the page containing Mockingbird Lane.

"Okay, I have it."

"See how small that print is?" the manager complained. "How is a guy my age supposed to read that?"

"I don't know, sir," Scooter chuckled nervously.

"Well, what does it say?"

"Page 30, J–8, whatever that means," AJ jumped in.

"Page 30, J–8, huh?" the man repeated. He then flipped to the front of the book and turned to page 30, which was a close-up map of half of Ridgetop Boulevard. The map was split into little squares. Down the side were letters A through K, and across the top were numbers 1 through 12. The manager put his finger on the letter J and then ran his finger to the right until it was in column 8.

"J–8, here it is." He lifted his finger up. In the square where his finger had been, we could see a bunch of roads, one of them being Mockingbird Lane. "Ah, there's Mockingbird. Thanks!"

6-1 13-1 7-5 3-3 11-4 1-9 12-2 45 10-6 2-2 7-1 4-5

The manager grabbed the map book and walked back to the counter, where he got on the phone to give directions to his driver. The four of us began to chuckle. Hopefully, it would be a long time before our eyes got that bad. No one said anything for a long while after that—we were busy stuffing our mouths with delicious pizza.

As we finished up lunch, I glanced over at Scooter and found him with his thinking face on, half-frown and half-smile at the same time.

"What are you thinking about, Scoot?" I asked.

"Oh, nothing. Just dreaming," he said. He was lying; I could tell. I figured he must not want to say something in front of Traverna Lynn.

"Well, then I guess we should head home, keep you from falling asleep on your bicycle," I joked. I was trying to hurry things along so we could head home and drop Traverna Lynn back at her apartment. Then, hopefully, I could discover what Scooter was really thinking about.

AJ patted his belly. "Well, we could ride our bikes home, or we could just roll ourselves home, I am so stuffed!"

As were all of us. In fact, the ride back uphill to the Birdcage was painful both to the legs and to our stomachs because we were so completely stuffed with pizza.

After saying goodbye to Traverna Lynn, we decided it would be easier to just walk our bikes up to our houses, rather than try and slowly ride up the hill. "Okay, Scoot, spill it," I demanded. "I know you got some great idea rattling around in that head of yours. Fill us in."

"No, it is still forming right now. Let's hurry up and get home so I can see if my theory is correct."

I wasn't even going to try and push him for a more detailed answer than that. I knew better; that was all the information I was going to get. That made for an anxious and long walk up the rest of the hill. But I'm glad that's all I knew at the time. If I had known just how great Scooter's next idea was going to be, the walk home would have been unbearable.

11-1 3-2 9-9 8-5 3-3 12-5 1-15 5-8 6-4 11-4 2

CHAPTER 10
Message Received

When we got to Scooter's house, AJ and I headed straight to the shelter while Scooter went inside his house to "get something."

The faint smell of paint could still be detected as we entered HQ, but it was so much better than the last day or so. Scoot had left the lid cracked again the night before, and apparently two nights of extra ventilation was just what HQ had needed. Speaking of Scoot, he arrived just a few moments after we did, and he was carrying his new copy of *The Adventures of Sherlock Holmes*. Without saying a word, he grabbed a blank sheet of paper from the printer tray and went over to the small, round table. He opened up the book to the page where the bookmark had been. He wrote down an *I* on the blank piece of paper, followed by a *G* and then a *U*, then *ESS*. His writing was very slow at first, but he had apparently cracked the code, because he started writing down letters faster, all the while getting more and more excited.

I could tell he was excited because he started getting "happy feet," which means he only has one foot on the ground at a time. It basically makes him look like he has to use the bathroom really bad.

After about five minutes of dancing and writing, he stepped back to reveal the whole message he had written out:

IGUESSCONGRATULATIONSAREINORDER?B UTIFYOUKNOWWHATISGOODFORYOU?YOUWI LLJUSTSTICKTOREADING?A?F?

"That's a lot of question marks!" AJ exclaimed. "What kind of message is that?"

"Oh, those are actually my question marks," Scooter explained. "Those mean I am not sure what is supposed to go there."

"Huh?"

"Let me back up and explain," Scooter answered. "I sort of figured this out while we were still at Seabeck Pizza. Remember when the manager asked us to find J–8 for him? Well, J–8 was sort of like an address. Go down to row J and then across to column 8. Now, look at this code. Most of the numbers come in pairs, just like the map in the book that we were looking at. So take the first pair of numbers, *23–8*. I went down twenty-three lines and over eight letters and got the letter *I*. Then I went down four lines and over fifteen letters to get the letter *G*, and so on and so forth. When the code goes to a new page, you just use the new page as your new map. But look, some of the numbers are not in pairs. I am

1-2 6-1 7-2 15-1 4-9 12-4 2-2 4-8 7-7 15-5 3-1 12-1

not sure what those mean, so I just put in a question mark for now."

I looked at what Scooter had written on the piece of paper. Clearly, the words to the message required some spaces to separate them. As I mentally put spaces in between the words, I realized that right where there should be a comma in the message, there was a single number (not a pair) in the code. It was just the number 7, all by itself. I looked at the top line of the page and noticed that there was a comma after the seventh word. I quickly looked for any other single numbers. There was a *14*, a *2*, and another *2*. Right after the fourteenth word was an exclamation point, and after the second word was a period. *That couldn't just be a coincidence, could it? I wondered.*

I quickly put spaces into Scooter's scribbling and added the punctuation according to my guesswork to form this completed message:

I GUESS CONGRATULATIONS ARE IN ORDER, BUT IF YOU KNOW WHAT IS GOOD FOR YOU, YOU WILL JUST STICK TO READING! A.F.

The three of us looked at the message I had just written and stared in silence for a long time. As usual, AJ was the first to speak up. "So, is your secret admirer just trying to make a joke or tease you or something?"

"I don't think so, Aidge," Scooter replied. "I don't even know anyone with the initials A.F. And I don't think they are joking, I actually think this was sent

8-3 3-2 14-4 5 11-3 18-1 15-7 17-1 6-6 15-6 8-12

as some sort of warning to back off. You know: don't try solving crimes, just stick to reading about them."

"Oh okay, Mr. Paranoid!" I laughed. "I bet this is from some kid at school who doesn't want you to get a big head about things and just wants to give you a hard time. You know, like I could say, 'AJ should just stick to hanging out with girls his own age and give up on chasing my sister, who won't give him the time of day.'"

AJ turned a little red, and Scooter and I got a good laugh.

"Well, I guess the only way we find out who is right is to figure out who A.F. is," Scooter said. "If we need it, I have my yearbook at the house. I could go grab it, and we could check to see if anyone from school has the initials A.F."

"We don't really have time; it's almost 5:30," AJ said, looking at his watch. "Almost time for dinner."

"Okay, but really quickly: can you think of anyone who rides our bus with the initials A.F.? They have to live close by. Remember that they put this book in my mailbox; they did not send it to me. So they must be close by." Scooter was starting to get excited again.

"Whatever, I gotta head home," I said. "We're supposed to get a call from my dad right after supper, and I don't want to be late or miss it."

"Okay, Ty, then why don't you check yearbooks later tonight. I will do a little digging for anyone outside of our school with the initials A.F. And AJ?

12-4 6-10 2-9 14-3 17-1 16-3 12-5 7-4 12-2 8-8 1-6 6-4

You do whatever it is you do." We all sort of chuckled at that one as we packed up and headed to our respective homes.

Luckily, I got home just in time for dinner. I wasn't starving or anything (Seabeck Pizza wasn't long ago), but I know if I had missed dinner without calling, it would have kickstarted that long lecture about responsibility and never being home and who knows what else.

After a quick supper, we sat down in the living room and talked while we waited for my dad to call. He was right on time, calling at 7:00 sharp. As usual, I got to talk to him first, because once my mom and sister were done talking to him he joked that his ears were quite full. He rarely talked about himself; he just kept asking questions about me and how things were going at home. My dad was always such a good listener. I told him about our broken bicycle case and how Scooter had gotten a sweet leatherbound book from a secret admirer. (I left out the part about the code. I wasn't sure if we were dealing with a jokester or a real, live threat, and I didn't want Dad to be sitting out in the middle of the ocean, worrying about me.) He gave his typical warnings about being careful and told me he loved me, and that was it. My turn was over.

As my older sister Tamara jumped onto the phone and began telling dad about her latest girly slumber party, I took that as my cue to leave and headed

26 8-1 9-2 1-4 16-1 19-6 5-4 26 14-29 15-2 6-3 2-11

upstairs to my room. Once I got to my room, I dug around in the closet until I found my yearbook. I had looked at it fairly recently, but it had gotten buried by all the dirty clothes I had tossed in the general direction of the clothes hamper. By the time I had found the yearbook, most of the clothes that had been on the floor were now in the hamper. I guess my mom would be happy I had to search for my yearbook!

I dove onto my bed and started looking to see if anyone at my school had the initials A.F. No such luck. Well, actually there was one person—Amanda Foster, but I gotta tell you, I was pretty sure she wasn't smart enough to come up with the code we found in Scooter's book. I got distracted by reading all the little notes people had written in my yearbook and didn't even notice when my sister entered my bedroom doorway.

"Missing school already, huh?" she asked jokingly. She knew better.

"Nah, just reading junk people wrote. Say, do you know anyone with the initials A.F.? Someone from school maybe? Or someone who lives in the neighborhood?"

"Hmm," she said thoughtfully as she looked toward the ceiling for an answer. "I don't think so... why?"

"Oh, no reason. I... just saw those initials carved into a tree while we were tromping through the woods," I lied.

10 3-3 15-7 10-2 12-5 18-2 9-5 16-9 16-10

"Nope, can't say that I do." She turned and headed across the hall to her own room and shut the door.

I was having no luck on my search for A.F. So I hoped perhaps AJ or Scooter would have better results when we met up in the morning. It was still pretty early for bed since it was the summertime, so I laid there in bed and picked up the Hardy Boys novel I had started a couple nights ago. I followed Frank and Joe around for who knows how long, until I couldn't do it anymore—I fell fast asleep.

CHAPTER 11
It Happened Once Before

Waking up in your clothes from the day before is always a little bit of an awkward experience, but I got over it quickly. Somehow, my book ended up on my nightstand, and my light got turned off. Thanks, Mom, I guess.

I took a quick shower to make it feel more like morning and then went downstairs. I wolfed down a bowl of Grape-Nuts topped with four and a half spoonfuls of sugar, tossed my bowl into the sink, and zipped out the door on my way to Scooter's house.

As I walked toward Scooter's house, I saw, to my horror, a police car parked in Scooter's driveway. My mind raced back to a couple months ago. While investigating the Old Man in the Mailbox case, we had come home one day after school to see the same thing—police in the Parks' driveway. That was not a good day. I hoped that somehow today would turn out better.

A lump filled my throat as I walked past the police cruiser. I tried to stay calm as I rang the doorbell. When Scooter came to the front door, who did I see standing behind him but Commander Coleman!

"Hey, Ty," Scooter said.

"Hi, Tyler," Commander Coleman said with a smile. "I was just leaving, but it is good to see you again." He stretched out his hand and shook mine. He then gave Scooter a stern look. "Remember what I said, Scooter. This is dangerous." With that, he walked away, got into his car, and slowly drove off.

"What was that all about?" I asked.

"Let's head down to HQ, and I will fill you in. AJ just called, and he is on his way."

A few minutes later, all three of us were inside the shelter. AJ had brought some soda and a couple packs of pudding cups with him, and he was putting them away in the fridge while Scooter and I plopped ourselves down on the couch. As AJ walked over, devouring a pudding cup, Scooter began to fill us in on his conversation with Commander Coleman. Apparently, a police report had been filed because someone had broken into an outdoor shed and trashed the place. It looked like someone had taken a sledgehammer that they'd found inside the shed and used it to break window panes, dent up a lawnmower, break a bunch of potted plants, and smash up the tires of a mountain bike.

"When Coleman heard there was a bicycle involved, he knew it was just a matter of time before we heard about it," Scooter said. "He came over to warn us that if this police report was connected in any way to our current case than we had better be careful, or better yet, let it go completely. He was warning us that it is getting dangerous."

"So do you think it is?" AJ asked.

"Is what?" Scooter replied, confused.

"Is this incident related to our case?"

"I don't know," Scooter answered. "He wouldn't even tell me where this happened. He is trying to steer us away from this story, not toward it."

"Are you sure about that?" I said half-jokingly. In the back of my mind, I wondered if Commander Coleman were really trying to get us to dig deeper.

"You know, maybe we can still figure out where this happened." Scooter got up and went over to his computer. "If there was a police report, there is a good chance it will show up in the police blotter in the newspaper, so I am going to check online now."

A couple clicks later, he leaned back and clapped his hands. "This is probably it. The article says, 'Police responded to a call on Thackery Place in the Thackery Hills housing development. Reports of breaking and entering with minor property damage to an outdoor structure were filed.' That sounds like it could be what Commander Coleman was talking about, doesn't it?"

"Sure does!" AJ said excitedly. "Where is Thackery Hills anyway? Maybe we can go check it out!"

2-4 9-6 4-5 15-3 10-7 13-11 6-4 11-5 14-4 10-2 18-3 8-8

"Wait, did you say Thackery Hills? Isn't that where James Killroy lives?" I asked.

"You know, I think it is," Scooter answered. "Maybe we should call him and see what he knows, see if he saw or heard anything last night." He picked up the phone and dialed the number from memory. Of course Scooter would have James' number memorized; James was a pretty good friend of ours and a member of our afterschool football gang. Unfortunately, our weekly football games had sort of fizzled out during the summer, since so many of the gang were on vacation. Bummer.

"Hey, James! How is the reigning mountain-bike champ doing?" This got a hearty laugh from AJ and me. Scooter listened for a minute, and his smile slowly disappeared into a scowl. "Really? Wow, we just heard about it from a friend in the police department. I was actually calling to see if you had heard anything about it, but obviously you have! I am sorry to hear that, man... Well, if we happen to swing by later, will you be there? We might want to check out the crime scene... Oh, okay, we will talk later, then." He hung up, shaking his head. He turned to speak to us.

"Apparently, it wasn't just James' neighborhood; it was the shed behind his house! He said his bicycle is pretty messed up now. He was about to run into town to get it fixed, but he said he would be back at the house later this afternoon if we wanted to check out the crime scene."

"Wow," was all that AJ could manage to say.

"Yeah, exactly," Scooter said, still shaking his head.

"You know, I don't think it's a coincidence that the night after James wins a bike race is when his bike gets destroyed, do you?" I asked. "I know Rick is upset about losing, but do you think he is capable of doing something like this?"

"I don't think so," Scooter said. "Rick is the kind of guy who would sabotage your bike beforehand to make sure that he won, but not the kind of sore loser who would destroy your bike afterward just because you beat him."

"I don't know about that," AJ jumped in.

"If he were a sore loser, he would have tried to wreck AJ's bike too, since AJ also beat him," I suggested.

"Good point!" Scooter said. "AJ, did you notice anything out of the ordinary at your house this morning?"

"Not that I know of," AJ shrugged his shoulders, "but I wasn't really paying attention."

That sounds about right, I thought to myself. "Well, I guess we better go check it out, then," I said aloud.

"Okay. You two head on over. I will lock up and catch up with you. I am going to grab my bike and meet you over there," Scooter said.

"And after we check out AJ's bike, I say we head over to the Track and see what Rick Rain has to say for himself," I suggested.

10-3 3-3 14-1 7-13 12-1 2-11 19-7 6-1 13-5 16-4 8-3

AJ and I took the shortcut through the woods behind Scooter's neighbors' houses. The trail dumped us out right across the street from AJ's house. As we walked up AJ's driveway, Scooter came pedaling up the street behind us.

Before we opened the garage door, we looked closely at the door to make sure it had not been tampered with. Nothing. Only then did we open the door and check out AJ's bike. It was hanging upside down by the tires from two hooks screwed into the ceiling. AJ rode his bike almost every day, but he still hung his bike up in that spot every time he was done with it. He sort of took pride in the fact that he could grab his bike, easily lift it, flip it above his head, and then hang it on the hooks. After Scooter had had a chance to thoroughly look it over before it was touched, AJ grabbed the bike and, with one swift and easy motion, brought the bike down with a flip and set it down on the tires.

"I think it is safe to say that nothing happened to your bike last night," Scooter said matter of factly. I think he was also a little disappointed.

"So where does that leave us, then?" AJ asked.

I spoke up. "I say we go down to the Track, see if Rick is there, and see what sort of reaction we get from him when we tell him about James' bicycle."

We all agreed to the plan, so we closed up AJ's garage and then went two houses down the road to my house so I could grab my bicycle. Then we headed down the street to the Track.

5-2 10-4 31 5-4 8-5 12-3 17-5 4-2 12-8 3-3 9-5

CHAPTER 12
Don't Be a Sore Loser

The Track, as we like to call it, is a retention pond located near the entrance to our Westridge neighborhood. It was built to hold all of the extra rain the neighborhood gets in the winter, but during the summer, there's not a drop of water in the place. So a bunch of us kids turned the large dirt bowl into a bike track equipped with a couple of dirt mounds used as jumps. Now, racers can go around inside the oval-shaped bowl while their friends stand on the rim to watch and cheer.

When we got to the track, Rick was there, all right. He was sitting on his bicycle, perched on top of a grassy mound that overlooked the bowl, watching a couple of kids racing. He saw us coming from a good distance away and yelled at us before we could even approach him.

"Hey, AppleJacks, I want a rematch!" AppleJacks was Rick's favorite nickname for AJ.

"I've told you that's not my name!" AJ shouted back.

"I know, but what else am I supposed to call you if I don't know what AJ stands for?"

"Uh, how about *AJ*? Since that's my name!" AJ said.

"You know, if you really want a rematch, maybe you should ask nicely," Scooter added.

"Fine," Rick said sarcastically. "Would you please do me the honor of a rematch, dear sir? Four laps will probably work."

"Four laps will be plenty of time to whoop you again," AJ answered.

"Great. If you need to warm up, you better do it now. We're racing soon as these two punks are done!"

"I don't even need to warm up to beat you!" AJ said.

A voice came from behind us: "So do you think a different bicycle is going to help you win this time?" We turned around to see Traverna Lynn walking her bike toward us. "That's a different bicycle than the one you used for the Silver-Days Race."

"You're right, it is!" AJ said. "I didn't even notice."

"Hey, Traverna Lynn," I said. "What brings you here?"

"Well, I was coming up here to do some investigating myself. Then I heard this guy yelling for AJ, and so I thought I would come say hi to you guys."

"She brings up a good point, Rick," Scooter jumped in. "Why are you using a different bike? Did yours not survive the crash when you ran into AJ?"

"The *back* of AJ to be more specific," I said.

9-12 8-9 2 5-4 16-6 12-4 11-2 16-1 18-6 8-3 11-3 6-1

"N-no!" Rick stammered, turning red with embarrassment. "When I went to go get my bike this morning, both tires were completely flat. So I had to use my old bike."

"Where were you keeping your bike?" Scooter asked.

"In the shed behind my house—why?" Rick asked, confused.

"And was this bike in the shed too?" Scooter pointed at the bike Rick was now seated on.

"No. It was buried under some junk in my garage. Why all the questions? Are we gonna race or what?" Rick was getting frustrated.

"I am asking because we are investigating a bunch of bikes that have been tampered with. Maybe yours was too," Scooter explained.

"Dude, it's just flat tires. Stuff like that happens."

"But both tires going flat at the same time? That sounds like someone might have gone into your shed and caused those tires go flat."

"Hey, Mister Detective! I know you're looking for your next big case and all, but there is no case here. I think I would know if someone broke into my own shed. I'm not an idiot!"

"Are you sure?" I whispered under my breath.

"I tell you what," Scooter said, "if AJ wins this race, then you take us to your house to take a look at your bike in the shed. If you win, then I will carry your bike over my head all the way to your house."

Rick laughed, "You're on! I can't wait to watch

those scrawny arms turn to rubber before we even get there!" He rode down the grassy mound and headed toward the starting line.

"Are you crazy?" I asked Scooter.

"Probably," he laughed nervously. "But either way this race goes, we will know where Rick lives, and we can do some snooping later if we need to."

"That is assuming you actually make it that far," I said.

"He can't live too far away; after all, he rides our bus. But I don't want to have to worry about it, so, AJ, just win! Please!"

Scooter, Traverna Lynn, and I turned to face the Track while AJ rode off to join Rick at the starting line.

I would like to tell you that the race was somehow exciting to watch, but it wasn't. One of the kids from the previous race gave the "Ready, Set, Go!" and the race began. AJ took off like a lightning bolt, but Rick fumbled with his pedals since he wasn't used to the bike. He was already way behind by the time he got going. AJ never looked back, and Rick never even had a chance to catch up. The race was pretty much over the moment it started.

Of course, Rick was ready with plenty of excuses. "You know I woulda beat you if I had my other bike," he whined.

"No, we don't know!" I joked. "When are you going to show us?"

"Just wait, Ty-Lurch (another horrible nickname).

13-2 14-5 4-6 11-3 30 8-11 16-1 14-9 20-5 9-1 2-2

This isn't over," he grumbled.

"For now, it is!" Scooter said. "Now it's time to show us your bicycle."

"Fine," Rick said with a huff. "C'mon, let's go." He rode his bicycle out of the dirt bowl and onto the main road of the neighborhood.

Well, Scooter's logic proved to be pretty solid. Rick Rain lived only a couple blocks from the Track. Scooter might actually have been able to carry Rick's bike that far, but I'm sure he was grateful that he didn't have to. The five of us ditched our bicycles in the driveway and headed around to the back of the house to check out the bicycle that was left in the shed.

"The shed" was not at all what I was expecting. I expected to find an aluminum shed, like so many people seem to have in their backyard or on the side of their house. Those sheds look like miniature barns. Rick's shed looked more like it had been built from what was left after someone had torn some old barn down. Most of the wood looked very old and cracked, and the two or three different colors of paint were extremely faded. The spacing between the boards was large enough that near the top of the shed, you could actually see daylight coming through from the other side. Based on how new they looked, the door hinges had clearly been replaced, but the Rains probably should have just replaced the whole door. The boards formed an uneven bottom with gaps so large a stray cat could crawl through. It took all my effort to hold in my laughter.

The door was held shut by a small wooden block that turned sideways. Rick turned the block, and the door began to creak open on its own. Once inside, it took a little time for my eyes to adjust to the darkness, but then I could see that the shed was full of garden tools, hoses, pots for outdoor plants, and of course, Rick's bike. Even from across the room with bad lighting, I could see that both tires were completely flat.

I whispered to AJ, who was standing next to me, "I'm not sure you would notice any property damage in here."

Traverna Lynn walked over and began examining the bike. In no time at all, she stood up. "Yep, this was definitely tampered with."

"How do you know?" Rick asked defensively.

She lifted the back tire for all to see. "See this tear right here? That's where your tire went flat, but it's on the side of the tire—not on the bottom, where you would normally get a flat tire. So someone must have poked the side of your tire with a screwdriver or a pair of scissors or something. There is an identical tear on the front tire."

"Wow, I can barely see that!" Rick exclaimed. "How did you even catch that?"

"That is sort of what she does," Scooter admired. "She notices things."

Traverna Lynn beamed. "Hey, what can I say?

10-1 9-2 8-8 7-4 6-5 11-9 14-4 19-1 37 16-9 4-2 2-7

Even a blind squirrel goes nutty every once in a while."

AJ and I laughed. Rick looked confused.

"That's also what she does," AJ joked. At that, we all laughed and filed out of the shed into the daylight and fresh air.

Rick was the first to speak once we got outside. "Well, I guess I owe you some thanks. I'm not sure I woulda even noticed someone had been in my shed."

"How could you—" AJ began to joke, but I gave him a hard elbow in the ribs, with a smile, of course.

"I think since your shed was unlocked," Scooter said, "the bike vandal we are chasing just went inside and popped your tires." He then went on to explain all about James' bicycle and the theory that perhaps the vandal was out to destroy the bikes of the competitors in the Silver-Days race.

"You really think my break-in is somehow connected to James'?"

"It has to be! You both finished in the top three of your division at yesterday's race. Now, one day later, both of your bikes have been vandalized? That can't just be coincidence," Scooter concluded.

"Boy, if I ever find out who did this, I'm gonna..." He trailed off before finishing his thought aloud. Then, pointing at AJ, he said, "What about AppleJacks here? He finished in the top three. Shouldn't his bike be broke too?"

"Yes, it should," Scooter said, "but AJ's bicycle was pretty much inaccessible last night. I think our

9-2 2-5 18-1 9-1 14-4 15-4 1-11 17-5 15-7 23

vandal went for easier targets instead. But we are going to change that: I have a plan."

"Huh?" Rick said, confused.

"Don't worry, I will let you know if it works," Scooter said with a laugh. "Come on, guys. I will explain on the way." He hopped onto his bicycle and began riding off.

"He's got a plan," I parroted with a smile, trying to frustrate Rick.

"Wait! What plan?" Rick asked angrily.

AJ and I began to ride off, leaving Rick just standing there and wondering what was going on.

"Am I coming too?" Traverna Lynn asked before we had pedaled too far away.

"I don't know, are you?" Scooter shouted back.

"Yes, I am!" Traverna Lynn said, accepting his coy invitation—as weak as it was. She hopped onto her bike and pedaled quickly to catch up with the three of us as we headed toward our end of the neighborhood. Rick just stood in his driveway and watched us ride out of sight.

1-2 17-10 13-3 9-6 5-1 6-5 18-15 9-5 6-1 5-1 9-9 14-5

CHAPTER 13
The Trap is Set

Scooter led us to his house. It was getting close to lunchtime, and Mrs. Parks was making waffles for lunch. Waffles are more of a breakfast food, for sure, but the visit from the police first thing that morning had sort of tossed the morning routine out of the window. So breakfast was sort of thrown together, and waffles got bumped to lunch. I didn't mind; I love waffles. The only hard part is trying to get a little butter and syrup into every little square of the waffle, especially if others are watching and waiting for you to pass the syrup when you're done.

By the time lunch was over, there was not a scrap of waffle left anywhere—except on Traverna Lynn's plate. She had almost a full waffle still sitting there.

"What is the matter dear? Are you not hungry?" asked Mrs. Parks.

"Oh, no, I'm fine. I ate two waffles before I grabbed this one; I guess my eyes are just bigger in my stomach."

Mrs. Parks opened her mouth to say something, but then she quickly shut it and just smiled.

After most of the dishes were cleared from the table, Scooter's mom left the remaining cleanup to us, and she took Urpy upstairs, presumably to take a nap. Scooter then told us about his plan. We would leave AJ's bike outside the garage, where the vandal could actually get to it. Meanwhile, Scooter would set up some video camera to record the whole thing, and we would have evidence to hand over to the police. And that would make Commander Coleman very happy. After finishing cleanup, we headed over to AJ's house to put Scooter's plan into action.

Obviously, AJ was not too thrilled about the idea of his bicycle being used as bait, but Scooter convinced him that there was no other way. And since we would have the vandal on videotape, it would be easy to get that person to pay to fix it once they were caught. Traverna Lynn suggested that we use a different bike as bait so that AJ wouldn't have to worry about his getting damaged. But Scooter pointed out that AJ's bike was too distinctive; if someone were out to break his bike, they would not be fooled by a cheap stand-in.

Scooter had a point there. AJ had one of the sweetest bicycles in all of Kitsap County. It was painted with this two-toned metallic paint; if you looked at the bike from the rear, it looked like it was a deep purple, but as you walked around the bike, it slowly seemed to change colors so that when you stood in

10-1 8 6-3 16-3 17-7 7-1 3-4 12-6 15-3 2-11 8-3 12-2

front of the bike, it looked like the bike was teal-blue. Coolest. Paint-job. Ever.

We decided to chain AJ's bicycle to the basketball hoop on the side of the driveway. That way, it wouldn't look like we were leaving the bike out as bait. Plus the basketball hoop was in such a place that Scooter could set up a camera inside AJ's house with a good view of the bicycle outside.

It was still the middle of the afternoon, but Scooter started the camera recording anyway, even though we didn't really think that the bike vandal would strike until that night. Once that was set up, we went to the backyard to waste some more of the afternoon. Since we were at AJ's house, he picked what we were going to do for the afternoon. He decided we would make a homemade obstacle course.

The last time we made an obstacle course, AJ had made it all about running around and climbing up on top of really tall stuff, pretty much guaranteeing himself the win. This time, we all took turns adding a piece to the obstacle course, so each person could add something they thought would favor their abilities. AJ went first, and he said we would start by running from the back porch to the far corner of the fenced-in yard. Scooter then said we would bear-crawl along the back fence, climb over the large doghouse, and then touch the other corner of the fence. I then took some of the firewood that had been stacked on the back porch and laid it on the ground,

14-1 16-2 11-3 8-5 11 9-4 5-4 14-1 7-7 4 7-4 8-4

with pieces about one foot apart, and I announced we would have to run across the firewood without touching the ground. Touching the ground would incur a two-second penalty. Traverna Lynn stated that next you would have to weave in and around the two clothesline poles in the form of a figure eight. We then took a couple more turns, each adding a couple more "events" to the obstacle course. I noticed that AJ used his turns to add running-type events, since he was obviously the fastest out of the four of us. Scooter and Traverna Lynn are both pretty small, so they added stuff that took advantage of that fact, like crawling under a picnic bench and weaving in and out of lawn furniture. Me? I couldn't think of anything that would particularly give me an advantage over everyone else, so I just picked crazy stuff that I thought would be hilarious to watch others do. So I chose, among other things, to have the racers climb over the fence, touch the ground on the other side, and then climb back over. No one, not even AJ, can climb a fence without looking ridiculous.

Once we had the obstacle course set up, we each took turns running, climbing, crawling, and jumping while we used AJ's stopwatch to clock our time. We let Traverna Lynn go first, and she posted a time of 1:57. Then Scooter got a time of 2:06. I was very tempted to harass Scooter for getting beaten by a girl, but I hadn't gone yet, so I decided I'd better keep my mouth shut. It was not a guarantee that I would beat her myself.

7-3 13-2 11-6 15-3 2-22 8-1 13-3 18-1 7-8 2-2 14-9 16-33

Next went AJ, and he actually clocked a time of 1:56. But he got a two-second penalty because he touched the ground while running across the firewood I had set out. So his final time was 1:58. Traverna Lynn still had the best time. Then it was my turn. Although I had picked climbing the fence because I thought everyone would look silly doing it, I did sort of have a strategy for how I would do it myself. Everyone seemed to take a long time to climb over the fence, so I was going to take a little extra time to get a running start and then jump to help myself over the fence. So that's what I did. While I was doing that event, I definitely *felt* like I was doing it faster than I had seen the others do it. I even backed away from the fence and took a running start to climb back over.

When I got to the back porch, which was the finish line, AJ announced my finishing time—1:40! I had crushed the previous best time, set by Traverna Lynn. Very satisfying, is all I can say.

Well, of course, AJ wanted another shot to beat my time, and the others chimed in that they did too. So I just sat on the back porch and became the full-time timekeeper while the three of them tried over and over to beat my time. Eventually, AJ adopted my strategy of getting a running start to climb the fence, and his times started getting much better. Finally, AJ posted a time of 1:38 and was ready to declare himself the winner. I was willing to call the competition over as well. But I was quick to remind

4-2 13-5 13-1 10-3 20-1 13-4 7-8 14-2 12-7 9-5 3

him that it had taken me only one attempt to get my time, and it had taken AJ more attempts than I could keep track of in order to beat me.

Everyone thought we should change up the course a little and race again. This time we took some more firewood and some wood planks (left-over from when we broke the fence the month before) and made a series of hurdles. Then we also added a soccer ball, which you had to dribble around the posts of the clothesline. I suggested that this time we do two laps through the course (just to mix it up even more), and surprisingly, they agreed. This gave me a huge advantage. I knew they had to be tired after doing the first obstacle course count-less times. I had only done it once, so I was feeling pretty rested.

Well, long story short, I won. After doing the two laps, I was huffing and puffing, so I knew the oth-ers would be downright exhausted. Sure enough, no one could beat my time the first go-around, and they quickly called it quits instead of trying again. Sweet victory! It is not very often that I beat AJ at anything that takes any athleticism, so I was quite proud of myself.

It was getting close to dinnertime, so Traverna Lynn said goodbye and rode off toward home. Scooter promised to keep her posted on anything new happening with AJ's bike. By the time we had the yard cleaned up, AJ's mom, Mrs. Seeva, had got-ten home from work. She had brought home some

19-3 3-7 11-7 15-7 16-6 21-1 21-2 5-6 13-4 3-7 10-6 1-6

Chinese takeout in anticipation of a quick dinner before she and Mr. Seeva had to leave again to attend some charity auction. Mr. Seeva then called to say he wouldn't even have time to come home before the auction, so Mrs. Seeva offered the three of us boys the dinner that had been meant for the whole Seeva family.

I called my mom to ask permission to eat at AJ's house. I made sure Mrs. Seeva was still around when I called, just in case I needed her to verify that she had indeed invited me and I had not invited myself over. Scooter then did the same thing. Shortly after that, AJ's mom had to go. That left the three of us boys to try and handle food with chopsticks on our own. Although I quickly gave up and resorted to a fork, dinner still took forever. But once we were done, we decided to hang out and watch a movie on AJ's big-screen.

When the movie was over, it was getting pretty dark, and so we decided to call it a night. As I was leaving, Scooter had me go out and check that the bicycle had not been tampered with while we weren't looking. I gave it a thorough inspection and concluded it had not. I discreetly gave Scooter a thumbs-up and then went on my way toward home. Scooter took this as his cue that nothing eventful was on the tape in the camera that had been recording while were away from the front of the house. He now felt it was safe to rewind and start recording again so there would be enough tape to record

39 11-5 5-5 5-3 16-5 17-1 10-1 3-8 15-9 2-1 1-3 12-1

through the night. Once he was done, he also headed home for the evening. We planned to meet in the morning at AJ's and see what our trap had caught.

7 2-1 3-8 3-3 2-23 2-24 1-3 2-6 1-10 1-25 7

CHAPTER 14
Time for a Little Drama

The next morning we checked out the bike, only to find it was in the same condition we had left it in—fortunate for AJ and his bike, but unfortunate for our case.

"Hmm" was all that Scooter could manage to say as he rubbed his chin and showed off his thinking pose. "I am quite surprised," he finally said after a long, thoughtful silence. "I really was expecting our vandal to strike last night."

"Maybe he needs more time," I suggested. "Another night of recording, maybe?"

"Perhaps," Scooter answered. "But I think maybe our vandal thought it might be too risky—with the bicycle being in front of the house, it was lit up by the streetlights. Or maybe it was too obvious that we were using it as bait. Man! I should have thought about these things yesterday!" He slapped his forehead with the palm of his hand. "You know, I just need some time to think. Let's head over to HQ and let me chew on this a little bit."

That sounded like a good idea to me. AJ felt the same way. So we quickly walked across the street and entered the woods on the shortcut trail that led to Scooter's backyard and HQ. Once inside HQ, Scooter hopped onto his computer and found that a few more messages had come in from The Network. It looked like the night before, while we were waiting for the vandal to strike at AJ's house, he instead was busy damaging two more bicycles. Scooter went to the map and added two more red Xs where the incidents had been reported.

"Man, The Network sure seems to be working well, doesn't it?" AJ asked.

"It sure does..." Scooter answered, trailing off as he got lost in his own thoughts.

"Too bad we always seem to be playing defense," I complained. "This vandal is always a step ahead of us. We'll never catch him if he doesn't make a bad mistake."

"So what do you think is our vandal's motivation? If it was to destroy all the bikes in the Silver-Days race, then why was he breaking bikes before then? And if it is just about destroying bikes, then it seems like a huge coincidence that he broke two of the top three finishers' bikes the day after the race they competed in. And why first and third place? Why would the vandal not go after second place too?"

"Maybe they are trying to frame me?" AJ said. "Trying to make it look like I did it, since my bike is the only one not broken."

"I doubt it," I said. "Everybody knows you and James are good friends. They would never believe you would do that to him. Now Rick Rain's bike? That's another story!" AJ and I chuckled.

Scooter was almost in a trance as he chanted seemingly random words: "Rick Rain... The Network... bike race... defense... offense." Suddenly, the light came on in his eyes, and I could see a great idea had just hit him.

"I've got it!" he exclaimed.

"You know why this guy is breaking bikes?" AJ asked.

"No, I am still working on that part," Scooter answered. "But I have a plan to catch him. And it is going to take a lot of people to pull off."

"Okay, spill it," I said impatiently.

"Okay, you know how in professional wrestling, they have the actual match, but they also have all the fake drama before and afterwards?"

"Yeah, I hate that part. It's so stupid," I said.

"Well, don't hate it too much, because we are going to create a little fake drama of our own! You think Rick is in a position to cooperate with us now?"

"Yeah, I think he is so ticked at whoever trashed his bike that he will do anything if it means we catch the guy," AJ answered.

"Good. Then this idea might work." Scooter went on to explain his plan. He figured the best way to

7-11 9-5 1-5 8 10-3 12-1 7-4 19-7 5-3 15-2

attract the attention of the bike vandal was to have another big race where lots of bikes would be present. Regardless of why he was breaking bikes, he would likely not be able to resist coming to at least watch the race. Since Silver-Days had just finished, there wouldn't be another big race for at least a month, and we couldn't afford to wait that long. So Scooter was going to put on a race of his own.

"But how do you get people interested in some race put on by a seventh-grader?" I asked.

"That's where Rick fits into the plan," Scooter said. Scooter was going to convince Rick to post on our Enigma Squad website how upset he was about losing the Silver-Days race and how he demanded a rematch. AJ and James would then respond publicly that they didn't want to. Then Rick would respond that only wimps would turn down a direct challenge. The argument would go back and forth, and finally AJ and James would accept. All of this would be on display for all to see on the website and hopefully drum up interest. Then Scooter would make an announcement on the website and via The Network about the upcoming race, and of course, they would get word out to the neighborhood.

"That sounds interesting, Scoot, but another race sounds like we're still playing defense," I said after he had explained the plan. "How will your idea be any different from what we've been doing so far? We still can't catch him in the act!"

"That is the second part of the plan, which I will

5-1 12-2 19-7 8-2 5-5 3-4 19-2 8-1 15-5 14-4 12-2 3-2

explain in a little bit," he answered confidently. "But let me set this part of the plan into motion first."

Scooter then called up Rick and James, and as predicted, they were both willing to do whatever we asked if it meant catching this bad guy. Scooter even got Rick to make his first trash-talking complaint on the Enigma Squad website while they were still talking on the phone. To make it a little more believable, Scooter made AJ wait a few minutes before posting a response.

In the meantime, Scooter drafted the email that he would later send out to The Network. The race would be two days later at the Westridge retention pond—better known as the Track—where AJ and Rick had held their mini-rematch. It would be eight laps, and the race would start at 3 p.m. To drum up more interest and make sure lots of people would bring their bikes, Scooter announced that starting at 2 p.m. and then every ten minutes after that, there would be a five-person, five-lap race. The winner of each race would win five dollars, courtesy of the Enigma Squad. Five dollars times six races was thirty dollars. The Enigma Squad luckily had that much money on-hand, thanks to some simple cases we had solved right after school had let out.

By the time Scooter had typed the email, it was time for AJ to respond to Rick's challenge. James would respond a half-hour later, per Scooter's instructions. The rest of the plan would go into motion over the next few hours just as Scooter had

3-1 9-2 18-7 14-2 8-4 2-1 9-1 5 11-8 18-4 7-14

laid out for us. AJ and James and Rick would feed off of each other and bad-mouth each other while, hopefully, the neighborhood looked on.

"So what about the other half of this brilliant plan?" I asked sarcastically as Scooter saved his email message to send later to all the members of The Network.

"Well, I am hoping we have a good turnout. I figure a chance to challenge your friends and win five bucks will bring tons of people out, and hopefully our vandal somehow hears about it."

"We already covered that part," I said impatiently. "I am interested in how we catch this guy."

"Oh, right. Sorry. Okay, here is where I hope we can go on the offensive and stop playing defense. So, a while back, our church held a 'used cell-phone drive' so that we could send the phones over to our missionaries serving in other countries. Well, some people turned in phones that were so old and obsolete that even the missionaries couldn't use them. My church was just going to throw them away, so I offered to take them. I figured they might come in handy someday.

"Well, a lot of the phones have a GPS chip inside of them for tracking the cell phone's location, and I have been working for a while on turning those little chips into tiny tracking devices. They will report their location to my computer every so often—however often I tell them to. I figure it's about time to try and put these to the test."

"So how do you plan on using them?" AJ asked.

"How many of these things do you have?" I added.

"I think I can have six or seven of them operational by the day after tomorrow," Scooter said confidently. "The plan is to bring Traverna Lynn to the race and, between the four of us, decide who we think the top suspects are. Then we place one of these devices on each of their bikes and trace their movements via my computer to see if any of their movements line up with future reports we get from The Network."

"So your plan is to cross our fingers and hope we get lucky?" I asked, feeling pretty skeptical. "Only six or seven tries to pick the bad guy? I don't like those chances."

"I think you will be surprised how many people we will be able to eliminate from consideration once you see who shows up. Plus, Traverna Lynn will be there, and she will be able to tell us if anyone who competed in the Silver-Days race shows up at our race. I think those people will be high on our suspect list."

"I still feel like we're just fishing," I complained.

"Of course we're fishing! If you have a better idea, I'm all ears!"

"No, I don't. I'm sorry. So what do we need to do next?"

"Um, the little trackers are not quite ready yet, so I have some work to do there. I don't know what you

6-4 16-8 10-5 15-2 1-12 6-11 36 2-7 11-2 19-3

guys should do."

Since Scooter did not have work for us to do, I knew exactly what I was going to do. The Seattle Mariners were playing an early afternoon game in Boston, which meant that the game would be late morning here on the West Coast. I turned on the radio so we could listen to the game and convinced AJ to play me in an epic game of Monopoly. The way we played, we changed a couple of rules, which almost guaranteed players could not lose all their money. Instead, the game ended when the bank ran out of money. Whoever had the most money at that point was the winner.

While Scooter worked hard getting his little tracking thingies to communicate with his computer, the Mariners beat the Red Sox, and AJ beat me at Monopoly—two things that rarely seemed to happen lately.

The rest of that day was pretty boring: Scooter kept tinkering, and AJ and I snacked all day and tried to fight the boredom. We didn't have very high hopes of anything happening, but we set up the camera and left AJ's bike out again that night as bait, just in case the bike vandal was behind schedule or something and would "get to it" a night later than we expected.

CHAPTER 15
Welcome to the Main Event

The next day started just like the day before. I had church in the morning, but I was too excited to wait. I got showered and dressed quickly, and while the girls in my house were getting all prettied up to go, I went down the street to see if anything had happened to AJ's bike overnight. Again, nothing had. I trotted back to my house and opened the front door just as mom was about to yell up the stairs for me to get downstairs. The confused look on her face was priceless! She stuttered for a sec and finally said, "Well, let's get in the car and go." Like I said, priceless.

After church I called AJ, and then we went over to HQ to check on Scooter. He was still tinkering, and it appeared he was going to be working on his stuff the rest of the day. That meant AJ and I were stuck trying to entertain ourselves. Finally, we decided to try and do something to spruce up the Track in order to get ready for the race. AJ and I spent the afternoon moving little rocks and twigs from inside the dirt bowl so racers wouldn't have to worry about them. Then we moved larger fallen branches and garbage away from where the spectators would be standing and sitting. We worked up quite a thirst from our work, which inspired AJ to suggest a great idea.

AJ's idea was to set up a table at the race and sell iced water bottles for one dollar a piece. We convinced my mom to pick us up a few cases of water and a couple bags of ice at the store while she was in town running errands. I promised to pay her back the next afternoon. I did the math. If we sold all seventy-five bottles of water, that would be seventy-five dollars. Subtract the twenty we needed to pay mom back for the water and ice, and we would have more than enough money to pay the thirty dollars to the winners of the races leading up to the main event. Nice thinking, AJ. I guess I can no longer say he never has any good ideas. Unless of course we hadn't sold any water, in which case it would have been the stupidest idea ever!

AJ and I successfully ate up most of the afternoon, and when we checked in with Scoot, he informed us that he had six tracking devices working and ready to go. He had even managed to create a silver cover for each of them so they looked like some sort of fancy gum wrapper at first glance. One side was sticky, so the devices could be attached to just about any surface.

15-7 4-5 2-12 13-1 15-8 14-7 46 7-4 11-14 6-6 11-8 3-3

After dinner, Scooter had AJ test one of the devices by sticking it to the underside of his bicycle seat and then riding all over the neighborhood for fifteen minutes. When AJ came back to HQ, Scooter was able to tell him almost exactly where he had been. We were ready. Now we just hoped for a good turnout at the race the next day. We would not be disappointed.

The races were supposed to start at 2 p.m., so we headed toward the Track a little after noon. AJ obviously had to take his bicycle because he was racing in the main event, but we also had to take a cooler with all the water bottles in it. So we set the middle of the cooler on AJ's bicycle seat, and then AJ walked his bike while Scooter and I kept the cooler balanced on the seat. Scooter and I both wore backpacks. Mine had extra bottles of water and a small box with money in it to pay the race winners as well as provide change for anyone who was buying water. Scooter's backpack held all the tracking devices and some fruit to snack on.

As we neared the Track, we could already see that we would have a fantastic turnout for the races. There were already at least twenty racers zipping around the Track. There were even a couple of cars parked on the street near the entrance to the retention pond. *Maybe we even got some high-schoolers to come?* I thought. *Or perhaps parents decided to come watch their child race?*

Once we got there, Scooter realized that we were

14-11 16-6 8-5 2-1 9-6 12-8 5-2 5-6 9-1 13-4 7-8

not nearly organized enough for the size of the crowd. He convinced one of the parents to drive him back to the Parks' home in order to pick up some more stuff. They returned fifteen minutes later with a card table, some paper and pens, a whistle, and a large orange traffic cone. I am not sure where Scooter got the traffic cone, but I figured the less I knew, the easier it would be to claim ignorance later.

Scooter set up the card table at the entrance to the Track and then put out some paper and pens. He was making a sheet for those who wanted to race, so they could sign up for one of the six races. He then went crazy blowing on the whistle to get everyone's attention. Once just about everyone had stopped moving, he stopped blowing on the whistle and picked up the giant traffic cone. He spoke loudly into one end of the cone, using it as a makeshift megaphone to make his voice louder.

"If you want to compete in one of the six races starting at 2 p.m., come sign up! You can only race once, and it is first-come, first-served. Also, we have bottled water for sale: one dollar each. Again, come sign up! At 1:45, you will be required to check your bike in unless it is your turn to race." He put the cone down, and many of the racers quickly formed a line at the table to get a spot in one of the races.

We had talked earlier, and the reason Scooter had told the racers they would need to check in their bicycles was twofold. First, fewer bicycles near the Track meant more people could fit along the edge

11-5 18-3 12-6 10-1 4-2 11-1 18-2 8-3 14-1 17-5 2-2

of the Track to watch the races. Secondly, if all the bikes were in the same spot it would be easier to keep an eye on anyone trying to mess with them. When Traverna Lynn got to the Track, the plan was to place her near the bike-holding area, where she could tell us if she saw anyone suspicious hanging around.

It was now 1 p.m., so we had a whole hour to mingle with the ever-growing crowd and look for the six suspects we planned to follow with Scooter's tracking devices. Actually, we didn't all get to mingle. I stayed at the table and helped with sign-ups as well as selling bottles of water. I hated to admit it, but AJ's idea was a huge success. The races hadn't even started, and we had already sold over half of the water!

Traverna Lynn showed up, said hello, and then quickly disappeared as she went to her lookout post, where she could watch who was hanging out near the bicycle check-in and holding area.

At 1:45 Scooter stopped by the table and said he would man the water table, if I would announce that all bikes should be checked in now and then run the races starting at 2 p.m. I agreed and, using the traffic cone as a megaphone, informed the crowd of over forty people that the first race would start in fifteen minutes. Standing near the starting line, I looked out at all the people who had shown up. Most were our junior-high friends from school, but there were many high-schoolers who showed up as

6-5 19-3 1-9 7-3 15-11 16-3 7-2 9-1 4-6 7

well. A few parents were there, either to cheer the kids on or make sure this many teenagers together in one spot weren't up to no good. With such a good turnout, I wondered if we might do this again later in the summer, but charge admission or something. It could be a little fundraiser for the Enigma Squad.

With this many people showing up, we had no problem filling up the five racing slots for each of the six races. Most of the racers signed up to be in the same race as their friends, so there were some really spirited races over the next hour. I was really enjoying myself. The next thing I knew, AJ, Scooter, and Traverna Lynn were standing next to me, ready to have a meeting. We had agreed ahead of time to get together as soon as the 2:50 race had started. This would give us just a few minutes to decide who the six suspects would be. Then while AJ was racing in the big race, the three of us would go plant the tracking bugs on our suspects' bicycles.

AJ was the first to speak up, or rather, whisper. "So there are a lot of people here. How are we going to narrow this down to just six potential bad guys?"

"Luckily, about half of those people are our friends. I think it is safe to eliminate them," Scooter said.

"Are you sure we can eliminate them as suspects just because they're your friends?" Traverna Lynn asked.

"Not based on that fact alone, no." Scooter seemed to have known that question was coming. "But all of our friends are junior-highers, and I am sort of assuming they would not have the freedom to be out late at night as often as would be required to pull off all of these vandalisms. I know it's a big assumption, but for now, I think it's one we have to make."

"So then that leaves a few adults and about ten or so high-schoolers to investigate," AJ said.

"Eleven, actually," Traverna Lynn said. "Exactly eleven."

"Are you sure?" AJ asked.

"Definitely," she answered. "You've got the guy over there in the blue Bermuda shorts, two kids over there in all black, the kid from the bike shop, the red-head wearing the 'I'm with Stupid' T-shirt, the—"

"Wait!" Scooter interrupted. "Did you say the kid from the bike shop is here? Where?"

Traverna Lynn pointed over toward the grassy mound that overlooked the whole track. Eddie—or "E-Free," as his menacing tattoo declared—was standing there on the rim of the bowl with a back-pack on his back, its strap crossing his chest from left shoulder to right hip. His right thumb was tucked under the backpack strap; his left hand was halfway buried in his pants' pocket. He was intently watch-ing the racers finish up the last of the preliminary races.

"I didn't see him earlier. When did he get here?" Scooter asked.

"He just arrived a couple minutes ago," Traverna Lynn answered.

14-3 9-6 18-5 3-3 4-4 12-5 13-2 17-5 8-4 7-13 5-6 11-10

"He's our guy," Scooter said confidently.

"What makes you say that?" Traverna Lynn asked. "He's not acting strange. He's acting just as normal as he did when he was looking at the bikes at the Silver-Days race."

"What? He was at Silver-Days, too? Oh, then he is definitely our guy!"

"Why is it so strange that a guy who fixes bikes would be at a bike race?" she asked, confusion written all over her face.

"I have been asking myself this one nagging question since we started this case: why? Why would someone go around breaking bicycles? What would they stand to gain? This guy definitely has something to gain from more broken bicycles—more business! Remember when we asked him if there was an increase in business lately? Looking back now, he sure was quick to say no, wasn't he?"

"So you think the only reason this guy has been breaking bicycles is simply to have more work to do?" I asked. "More broken bicycles means more work. His boss is the one who makes more money."

"Tyler, you think his boss is in on it?" AJ chimed in. "You think his boss is sending him out to drum up business?"

"I'm not saying any of that. All I'm saying is, Scooter's theory is pretty shaky."

"I am telling you, Mr. Eddie over there is our guy." Scooter was sticking to his story, I'll give him that. He reached into his bag and pulled out the small

18-1 17-3 12-4 2-4 9-6 5-11 3-1 11-1 10-3 3-2 15-5 8-9

trackers. "I'll tell you what: you guys follow which-ever five other people you want, but I am going to follow the one *real* bad guy. Now, which bicycle was he riding?"

"I don't think he was riding one. I think he might have walked here from... wherever he came from," Traverna Lynn said.

"Oh, great, that means we have to somehow get this thing to stick to his clothing," Scooter com-plained, holding up a tracker.

"Or maybe his backpack," AJ suggested.

"What if he changes clothes or ditches his back-pack before he breaks another bicycle?" I pointed out.

"That's a possibility," Scooter said. "I don't like it, but it's a risk we are going to have to take. Now, I am going to need help with this. Anyone want to come be a distraction?"

"Leave it to me," Traverna Lynn said with a smile.

The rim of the Track was lined with people, so Scooter and Traverna Lynn disappeared behind all the spectators and then reappeared a few moments later just a few feet away from Eddie. They walked casually along the rim toward Eddie, Traverna Lynn in the lead and Scooter following a short distance behind. When Traverna Lynn reached Eddie, she attempted to pass in front of him and then purposely misstepped and began falling into the dirt track. As she fell, she reached her hand toward Eddie in a plea for help. Eddie reacted the way anyone would with

2-4 11-3 18-2 7-2 14-3 12-2 6-4 8-4 7-5 9-3 16-6

only a split-second to think: he lurched forward and attempted to catch her hand. Traverna Lynn took a tumble onto the dirt inside the bowl. Eddie also fell into the bowl but stayed on his feet. Scooter came closer, holding out his hand to offer help, as Eddie and Traverna Lynn scrambled to get back up on the rim. Eddie grabbed Scooter's hand to climb back up, and as Eddie got up, Scooter reached around him to put his hand on the backpack, as if to steady Eddie. In the process, he stuck the tracker on the backpack. The boys helped Traverna Lynn back onto the rim, and I could see that she and Scooter made a little small talk with Eddie and then went on their way.

By the time they got back to me at the starting line, it was time for the main event. I tried to make the race seem as big a deal as I could when I announced each of the racers. AJ, James, and Rick did a good job of trash-talking even at the starting line to try and add to the drama.

I can't tell you much about the race because as soon as I blew the whistle to begin it, I had to run off with Traverna Lynn and place the other five trackers. All the kids were supposed to put their bikes back in the check-in area, so we headed that direction. I had to admit, I hoped that Scooter was right about Eddie, because we didn't have any idea who would make a good suspect otherwise. We ended up placing the five trackers on the bicycles of the five scariest-looking high-schoolers, hoping we would get lucky. All the more reason to hope Scoot was right.

39 7-3 11-7 14 10-7 14-4 4-4 8-2 9-10 13-3

We finished and got back just in time to see the racers finish: AJ, then Rick, then James. That seemed to make sense. The Track was located in AJ and Rick's neighborhood, so they had a little home-field advantage. It was good to see AJ still beat Rick, even if the race didn't really mean anything. The real purpose of the afternoon was to draw out the vandal, and if Scooter's hunch were correct, it may have done just that.

A few racers stayed behind, but the rest of the crowd quickly dissipated. Scooter went to the table to pay the race winners. When I got to the table, he had paid all the winners and was breaking down the card table. The parent who had helped him earlier had offered to drive Scooter and all his stuff home. I tried to help pack things up. I opened up the cooler to see we had sold all but two of the water bottles. This afternoon had turned out great in every way! That meant we had made money—even after paying the race winners and paying my mom back for the water and ice. I dumped the melting ice out of the cooler and tossed it into the backseat of the waiting car.

Traverna Lynn had to head back to her apartment, and AJ had already taken off somewhere with James. So once Scooter left in the car with all his stuff, I was left standing there all by myself. I looked over at the Track and smiled. *Good times.* I then turned and began the half-mile walk home.

14-5 16-2 3-6 5-3 2-8 9-3 17-2 172

CHAPTER 16
Someone is on the Move

I was starving by the time I got to my house, so I went inside to find something to eat. Anxious to see if the tracking devices were doing their job, I figured I would grab a quick snack before heading over to HQ. When I walked into the kitchen, I could see my sister in the living room, lying on the couch, watching some chick flick. I knew that if she saw me, she'd start asking all sorts of questions, and I didn't have time to answer them. I tried to find something in the cupboard that I could grab and run. The first thing I saw was a box of croutons. Something salty sounded good, and it would go well with something sweet—like the chocolate pudding I knew was in the fridge at HQ. I grabbed the box from the cupboard and snuck out of the house as quickly and quietly as I had come in.

I don't even want to guess what my neighbors must have thought, watching me walking down the middle of the street and eating croutons right out of the box. I was hungry, though, so I didn't care.

I assumed Scooter was already in HQ, so I didn't even bother to see if he was home. I just walked around to the backyard and headed for the woods and the Right Hook tunnel. As I suspected, Scooter was already there, sitting at his computer and watching a map on the screen. I said hello and then went straight for the fridge to find a pudding cup. I suddenly felt like AJ!

I found a spoon, started eating my pudding, and joined Scooter by the computer.

"Nothing too eventful so far—not that I really would have expected something until tonight, anyway," Scooter said. Unlike a normal map, which is mostly white with black lines, the computer screen was mostly black with white lines representing roads. There were six green dots that must have represented the tracking devices. Only two of them were moving, and those were moving so slowly that you almost couldn't tell they were moving at all.

"So which one is the bike shop kid, Eddie?" I asked.

"I don't know."

"What do you mean you don't know?" I asked astonished.

"That's just it: to try and remain objective, I decided to follow all six suspects blindly, without knowing which one is which. That way we go after the dot that exhibits the most suspicious behavior—whether that turns out to be Eddie or somebody else."

"Oh, okay. That's pretty smart."

"I know," he said with a smile.

Well, watching those green dots was about as exciting as watching paint dry. I lasted about two more minutes before I had had enough. I walked over to the couch and laid down. Come to think of it, I was sort of tired. I rested my eyes for a sec, and pretty soon I was fast asleep.

I awoke with an "OOF!" AJ was sitting on top of me! Apparently, I had been asleep for quite a while, and AJ had shown up sometime during my nap. They could have done much more to me while I was sleeping, so I guess I should be grateful that AJ decided to just jump on top of me and nothing else!

Once my heart finally stopped racing and AJ got off of me so I could sit up, I asked Scooter if he knew anything more than before I had fallen asleep.

"Well, we know which tracker belongs to Eddie. Shortly after you fell asleep, one of the little green dots on the screen moved toward Old-Town Silverdale and has been down there ever since."

"So you think that belongs to Eddie, and he went down to the bike shop to go to work, huh?"

"Yes, I think so. I guess it could belong to someone who is visiting the bike shop, but the dot hasn't moved for almost an hour and a half. So I doubt they would be there that long."

"Wait. What if someone needed their bike fixed? Since we put the tracker on the bicycle, they might be leaving the bike there until it was fixed," I argued.

Scooter pointed at the dot we were talking about.

"But if this is Eddie, then sometime after 7 p.m., it will move when he goes home; I am pretty sure I remember that the bike shop closes at seven. If it is someone else, then it will probably stay right there all night. Either way, we should have our answer by morning."

"Sounds logical," I concluded. "What time is it, anyway?"

"A little after 6 p.m.," AJ answered.

"Oh shoot! I'm late for dinner! My mom's gonna be ticked! I gotta jet!" I said as I headed for the door.

"Don't forget this," Scooter said as he handed me the cash box with the money from the water bottle sales.

"Right." I grabbed the box and headed toward the door again. "It'll probably be a good idea for me to stay home tonight, so I'll just catch up with you tomorrow."

When I got home, my mom was in the kitchen putting the finishing touches on the dinner casserole. Good. I was late by 6:00 standards, but I wasn't late for dinner. I told her I was sorry and that I had fallen asleep. Wrong thing to say. She forgave me, but not before giving me a lecture about how I must be staying up too late if I needed a nap the next day. I assured her this was not the case. I also paid back the money that she had loaned me for the water bottles and ice. She seemed genuinely surprised and impressed that we had sold enough to pay her back.

After dinner I volunteered to take Tamara's turn

at dish duty. I hoped that sometime in the future when I asked, she would remember that moment and return the favor. After I finished the dishes, I went upstairs and jumped back into my library book. Every time my body started to say, "Go to sleep," I would tell it, "Just a few more pages." After about the fifth time this happened, I finally gave in, turned the lights off, and went to sleep.

The next morning I woke up to my mom standing over me. One hand was on her hip, and the other was holding the cordless phone against her shoulder. She had a frown on her face. Apparently she was holding the phone that way so she could lecture me without the person on the other end of the phone listening in.

"What time did you go to sleep last night?" she demanded.

"I don't know. I was reading a book until I felt tired, and then I went to sleep."

"Well, maybe I need to set a bedtime for you!"

"W-wait. Why?" I stammered.

"I've been calling for you for three minutes! But apparently you're too tired to even hear me! Here." She handed the phone to me. "AJ has been waiting." Then she turned and stalked out of my room.

Note to self: make sure later to steer mom away from the whole curfew idea. I turned my attention to AJ on the phone. "Hey, Aidge! What's up?"

"Hey, Ty. My dad decided to take the day off

today and wanted to take all of us boys to the Kitsap Blue Jackets games this afternoon. They're playing a doubleheader. Are you in? Scooter already said yes."

"Of course! What time are you leaving?" I asked.

"My dad said we'll grab lunch in town somewhere before heading over to the games. So be at my house in fifteen minutes?"

"Fifteen minutes? What? Wait, what time is it?" I asked.

"Almost noon."

Oh, wow! I slept the whole morning away; no wonder my mom is so irritated. "All right, I'll be there as soon as I can," I told him and hung up.

I jumped out of bed and headed for the shower. I was hoping that while I was in there, my brain would start working and I could remember where I had placed my baseball mitt. There was a souvenir foul ball calling my name, and I was going to catch it today.

When I got over to AJ's house, Scooter, AJ, and Mr. Seeva were already standing in the driveway waiting for me. "Good afternoon, sleepyhead," AJ joked.

"Sorry to keep you waiting, sir," I said sheepishly to Mr. Seeva.

"No problem. The first game doesn't start until 2 p.m., so we have plenty of time to get something to eat. How does Azteca sound?"

"Mexican food sounds great!" I said. Scooter and AJ agreed. With that, we piled into the Seevas' sweet SUV and headed into town.

At the restaurant we placed our orders and then got busy pigging out on chips and salsa. Then AJ's dad got a call on his cell phone, and he said he just "had to take it" and excused himself to take the conversation outside. As soon as he was out of earshot, Scooter rummaged in his backpack and pulled out a computer printout.

"As I suspected, Mr. 'E-Free' Eddie was pretty busy last night. I set my computer to record where each of the tracking devices was throughout last night, and look at this." He showed us a map that had tons of times written on it next to a red line that went all over the map.

"So this map is a listing of everywhere this tracking device went and at what time." Scooter began his explanation in his annoying teacher mode. "See here, at 7 p.m., the device is still at the bike shop. Then at 7:10 p.m., it starts moving and it goes up to this location off of Ridgetop Boulevard. I think this is Eddie's house. Then at 9:30, he leaves and goes to three different locations over the next couple hours and then comes back to his home, where he stays the rest of the night."

"So did we get any chatter from The Network about bike vandalisms that line up with any of those three spots?" I asked, a little skeptical.

"Unfortunately, no," Scooter said. "But of the six trackers, only Eddie's moved after 9:00. There is no evidence yet that anything happened while Eddie was away from his house, but as my dad always says, 'Nothing good ever happens after dark.' And in Eddie's case, I imagine he has a valid point.

"Also, I noticed something else: look at where Eddie's house is. Look how close it is to the Birdcage. There isn't a road that goes from Ridgetop down to the Birdcage, but there is a paved bicycle trail that connects the two. Eddie would have pretty easy access to the Birdcage that way."

"And he wouldn't have to go through the main entrance and be seen by the security guards," AJ jumped in.

"See, it's all starting to come together," Scooter concluded.

"So what now?" AJ asked. Scooter was about to answer, but Mr. Seeva had ended his phone conversation and had rejoined the table. Our server was right behind him with a tray of sizzling fajitas. Without saying anything, we all knew we would pick this conversation back up during the baseball games.

The rest of lunch was pretty uneventful. We mostly let Mr. Seeva question us about what we had been up to with our summer free time. Mr. Seeva was always working late or at some fundraiser dinner, so his time with his son was pretty limited. Today was his attempt to spend some time with AJ and catch up.

After lunch we zipped on over to the county fairgrounds to watch the Kitsap Blue Jackets play a doubleheader. Normally the smell of grilling hamburgers and hotdogs would have my mouth watering, but I had successfully stuffed myself with fajitas and free chips and salsa. The normally tasty smells of the ballpark had no appeal since I was so full. But I still enjoyed plenty of the things that made me smile every time I went to the ballpark: the smell of cut grass, the cool designs the lawnmowers would cut into the outfield, the sunflower seeds and peanut shells strewn everywhere, the bright white chalk marking the field—so white that the lines actually appeared to be glowing. And of course the energy that sort of hangs in the air at the possibility of a foul ball coming my way at any moment.

After a few innings, Scooter nudged me and told me to follow him. I reluctantly left my prime foul-ball-catching spot and followed him to an area along the third-base line where anyone could stand and watch the game.

Scooter started in, "Okay, so about our plan..."

"Whoa, wait! What plan? What did I miss?" I interrupted.

"The plan to catch Eddie, the bike shop kid," AJ said.

"Wait, did I miss the part where you talked about the plan?" I asked.

"Yes, you did," Scooter laughed. "So as I already explained to AJ while you were busy daydreaming, I think we need to head over to Eddie's house tonight and see if we can dig up some sort of evidence before we turn this stuff over to Commander

Coleman. The tracker only gives us a pretty good idea of where Eddie lives, but we still need to narrow it down to the actual house. I have an idea for how to do that," Scooter said.

"Okay, so when are we going to do this?" I asked.

"Tonight, after dark. By the time these two ball games are over and we get home, it should be about time to head toward his house."

"Well, sounds like we should spend the night at AJ's house, then," I said. We had learned from experience that if we ever wanted to do anything late at night, we should spend the night at the Seevas'. AJ's parents would let us play outside after dark, and Scooter's and my parents would not worry about us if we were spending the night over there.

"I'll go ask," AJ said as he walked off to find his dad. Scooter and I followed. We would each have to make a phone call to our parents, assuming AJ's dad said yes.

Mr. Seeva was more than happy to say yes. Scooter's mom also said yes. My mom sort of reluctantly said yes. Then all three of us boys said, "YES!" The plan—as vague as it seemed—was set.

I easily distracted myself from worrying about our plan for the night. After all, there was baseball going on. I couldn't say the same for AJ and Scooter. They weren't as big baseball fans as me, and I could see they were just itching for the second game to be over.

Mr. Seeva sort of helped them out by getting

bored himself, and we ended up leaving at the seventh-inning stretch of game number two. I was okay with that: the Blue Jackets were ahead 14–5, so I felt pretty sure they wouldn't lose that lead if I left.

CHAPTER 17
House Hunting

When we got to AJ's house, it was a little after 8 p.m. Mr. Seeva said goodnight and headed upstairs to join Mrs. Seeva, who was watching TV. Scooter used AJ's home computer to check our Enigma Squad email inbox to see if we had gotten any messages from The Network. There was still no news about any vandalism from the night before. There was, however, a message from Traverna Lynn. She was checking in to see if we had any news. We talked about it briefly and then decided to let her join us for the night's activities if she wanted to. Scooter called her and told her about our plan. We were going to be dressed in our ninja uniforms, which just meant we would wear all the black clothes we could find, so Scooter told Traverna Lynn she should also dress for some "covert operations." We agreed to meet her at her apartment at 9:00.

Next, Scooter and I both went home to pick up overnight clothes, fresh clothes for the next day, and of course, our ninja garb for the evening's excursion. By the time we both got back to AJ's house, we had to rush in order to make it to Traverna Lynn's by nine.

Scooter had picked up his backpack while at his house and told us his "plan" was packed inside. We jumped onto our bikes and zipped down the hill to the Birdcage and Traverna Lynn.

When we got to the apartment, Traverna Lynn was sitting on the front porch, waiting for us. She was dressed in camouflage from head to toe! She apparently picked up on our sense of awe mixed with confusion when she saw the dumb looks stuck on our faces. She said, "My dad likes to hunt, and my sister would never even consider going with him, so I get to go with him often. Gotta dress the part when I go!"

We all laughed. Then our covert-ops training kicked in, and we fell silent as we started heading up the bike trail towards Eddie's neighborhood. If anyone were watching us, I'm sure they would have cracked up to see three ninjas and a short army commando walking bicycles up a steep hill.

When we got to the top of the trail, we took our bicycles and stashed them in some nearby bushes. We then crept through the neighborhood toward the spot where the tracker showed Eddie was spending a lot of time. Since the tracker was shown to be at this location more than any other during the night before, Scooter assumed that we were now in the area where Eddie must live. It sounded like a good theory to the rest of us.

We reached an intersection of two streets with a house in each corner. There was only one street-light directly above the intersection, so as we crept up the street, we were pretty well hidden by shadows. The house to our left had a huge apple tree in the front yard that actually hung out over the street somewhat. We crouched beneath the outstretched branches of the apple tree, gaining greater concealment from the tree's shadow.

"Well, this is it," Scooter said. "The tracker indicated this is where Eddie lives, so we have it narrowed down to these four houses." He pointed to the houses in each of the corners.

"You don't know which house is Eddie's?" Traverna Lynn asked. From our vantage point, we couldn't see anything that made it obvious which house belonged to Eddie. Each of the houses had landscaping that created eerie shadows and further blocked our view.

"No, the tracker only narrows down the location to this intersection," Scooter answered. "But I have a plan to find out." He took his backpack off his shoulder and opened it. I recognized the device as soon as he brought it into view. It was the car alarm that he had installed as a Distraction Device back at his house. He then dug into a side pocket and pulled out the remote control used to set off the alarm from a distance.

Although none of the four yards had fences, the

house on the far side of the intersection and to our left had some neatly trimmed hedges, which ran along the edge of the yard next to the road. The end of the hedge was almost directly beneath the lone streetlight. Scooter's plan was to have AJ pose as a late-night jogger and jog through the intersection. When he passed by the hedge under the streetlight, he would toss the car alarm inside the hedge and then just continue running through the rest of the intersection. When AJ was safe in the shadows of the trees on the other side of the intersection, Scooter would set off the alarm and let it ring until people came outside to figure out what was going on. He hoped, based on who came outside from each of the houses, that we could deduce which house belonged to Eddie.

AJ wasn't too excited about being the one who had to go out in the open and risk being noticed, but he got over it. He did exactly what Scooter asked. He jogged into the intersection as if he were out for a late night run, tossed the small alarm into the hedge as he jogged past, and then kept jogging until he was out of the reach of the streetlight. He then hunkered down in the shadows on the opposite end of the intersection. We could see him crouched down, but no one else would be able to see him unless they knew where to look.

Scooter pushed the alarm button on the key chain, and the alarm made a very loud *whoop-whoop* sound and then quickly stopped. Scooter looked confused.

Apparently, that was not what was supposed to happen. He tried to push the button again, but nothing happened.

"Shoot. The battery must be dead," he whispered.

The brief noise was enough to at least make a few dogs go crazy. We heard barking coming from two different houses, and we could hear a person from one of the houses yelling for his dog to calm down. Across the way we could see AJ with his hands out as if to say, "What now?" I shrugged my shoulders with a response of, "I don't know."

Scooter crouched silently for a moment, listening and thinking. Suddenly, he dug into his backpack again. He had an idea—I could just tell. He pulled a water bottle out of his bag and then crawled a few feet away and picked up an empty glass beer bottle that had been tossed into the grass along the street.

"Okay, time for plan B. We have dogs; we will use the dogs." He took the beer bottle and blew over the top of the opening so it made a low, steady tone. He then opened his water bottle and poured water into the beer bottle until it was half full. He blew over the opening and again it made a tone, but this time the pitch was much higher. He poured more water into the bottle and again made a tone, which was even higher. He kept doing this until the beer bottle was nearly full of water, and when he blew over the opening, it seemed to stop making any noise.

"So you know how dogs have really good hearing and can hear sounds that humans can't?" he asked.

"Yeah," I whispered. Traverna Lynn just nodded her head.

"Well, I am counting on that. The more water I put into this bottle, the higher the pitch. I am guessing that now that the bottle is nearly full, the bottle is still making a sound, but it is higher than we can actually hear. So here goes nothing."

He took a huge breath and then blew over the top of the bottle as hard as he could. All I could hear was the sound of Scooter blowing hard, but his idea must have worked because suddenly there were three or four distinct dogs barking up a storm! Scoot took a deep breath and started blowing again. Dogs continued to bark, and a few owners could be heard yelling for their dogs to be quiet. I am not really a dog person, but I'm not sure that yelling at your dog to be quiet is really the way to go. But what do I know?

Porch lights began to come on. The house immediately to our left flicked on the front porch light, and a man in his sixties opened the front door and stood staring out into the night. Unless Eddie were staying with his grandparents (which I guess was possible), this was probably not his house. That left three other possibilities.

Scooter stopped blowing, just in case he might be heard by the man who was just a stone's throw away. We laid perfectly still in the shadows, waiting for the old man to lose interest and go back inside. Meanwhile, the front door to the house diagonally across from us opened. The porch light never turned on, but we could see a large dog saunter off the porch and into the front yard. After about a minute, someone at the front door yelled at the dog to come back inside. It sounded like a teenager—in fact, it sounded like Eddie! I looked toward Scooter. He just nodded his head in agreement. He knew what I was thinking. The dog ignored instructions to "come here" and instead wandered farther away from the house. It eventually walked close enough to the streetlight that we could see it was some sort of Great Dane, a huge, muscular dog with spotted coloring. Eventually, the dog's owner walked off the porch, came over, and grabbed the dog by the collar. He came just far enough out from the shadows to confirm that it was indeed Eddie.

While we watched Eddie drag his dog back into the house, the old man near us went back inside and turned his porch light off. We felt like we could finally relax again. I looked across the intersection, and for some reason, I couldn't see AJ in his hiding spot. I began to worry for a second until I heard his familiar voice behind me. He must have circled around us by taking another street. "So now we know where Eddie is. What's next?"

Scooter began to outline the plan: "I think we should come back here tomorrow during the day. Eddie should be at work, and we can figure out how exac—" He stopped mid-sentence. The porch light to Eddie's house had just turned on. The front door opened, and a heavyset lady wearing nursing scrubs appeared in the doorway.

Although there was no way we could be seen in our hiding spot, the four of us instinctively crouched just a little lower and watched as she continued a conversation she must have been having before she opened the door: "—and put the dog outside before you go to sleep! I don't want another mess on the floor in the morning. If there is, you'll be the one cleaning it up!" She shut the door rather forcefully and then fumbled to find her car keys in the large canvas bag that was hanging from her elbow.

There were two cars in the driveway. One was a small compact car that was probably at least twenty years old. The paint was chipping everywhere, and the passenger door was a different color completely. That must be Eddie's car. The other car was a newer-model four-door sedan. The woman unlocked the car and climbed in. The car started right up and drove away.

I was about to turn and ask Scooter what he thought when the front door opened again. Eddie appeared, holding the Great Dane by the collar.

"That didn't take long," Scooter said with a knowing smile.

"What didn't take long?" AJ whispered.

"How much you do want to bet Eddie is about to head out for some late-night bicycle smashing?" Scooter said. "I am guessing that was his mom who just left to go to work. This is sort of what I figured was happening. This is why he can run around at night and not get in trouble. Nobody is home to notice he's gone. Just watch."

Sure enough, Eddie took the dog over to the right side of the house, where a large doghouse stood in the shadows. He hooked the dog up to a chain attached to the doghouse. *I wonder how long that chain is?* I thought to myself. I quickly got my answer. As Eddie walked back toward the open front door, the dog slowly followed. About halfway to the front door, the chain went taut, and the dog quickly lost interest in Eddie, turned around, and wandered back to the doghouse, where he plopped himself down. I guessed this was becoming a nightly ritual for him. Eddie reached inside the front door and grabbed his backpack and keys from some unseen hiding spot. He then shut the front door and locked it with his keys. He jumped into his car, and it started up with a very loud roar. He then pulled out of the driveway, turned away from us, rumbled down the street, and disappeared into the darkness.

We all sat there for a moment, digesting what had just happened. Finally, AJ jumped up. "Well, let's go check it out."

"Wait, how do we know no one else is home?" I asked.

"I am pretty confident that it is just Eddie and his mom living there, based on the conversation we just heard, but we should probably make sure," Scooter said.

I thought for a moment. "I know: I'll go up and ring the doorbell. If no one comes to the door, then we can assume the coast is clear. If someone does answer, well, then I'll make something up."

I stood up and started walking across the lighted intersection toward Eddie's front porch. The house was one story and shaped like a rectangle. Even with little light, I could see that the light-colored siding on the house was in need of a new paint-job. The driveway where the two cars had recently been parked ran along the right side of the house and ended at a garage, which was not attached to the house. As I walked up the front steps, I half expected the dog to go crazy and tell the whole neighborhood I was there. Instead, he just looked up briefly and then put his head back down on his front paws. Some guard dog.

I rang the doorbell and waited. I decided that if anyone did answer the door, I would just say a bunch of us kids were playing Capture the Flag in the dark, and we wanted to know if Eddie would like to join us. Then they would say, "Eddie isn't here." And I would say, "Okay, sorry to bother you," and then eventually a message would get back to Eddie that some kids were looking to play in the dark and he was invited. And he would probably be glad he wasn't around to answer the door. No harm done.

Fortunately, none of that conversation had to take place because no one ever came to the door. I'm not sure how long I stood there, but I finally turned around to give the "coast is clear" signal.

AJ, Scooter, and Traverna Lynn tried to remain in the shadows as they worked their way around the outskirts of the intersection and met me under the eaves of the front porch. Without saying a word, we walked around the left side of the house, away from the doghouse. Once we got around the corner, we found it was much darker because the house blocked the streetlight.

We all started looking at the windows. I was looking for which windows might be best to look into in the hopes of seeing if Eddie had left any evidence lying around. But that was not what everyone else was looking for.

There were three windows on this side of the house, and the middle window had been left open. A lot of houses in our town do not have an air-conditioner, because it only gets really hot enough to use one for a few weeks every year. So a lot of people cool their houses the old-fashioned way: leave a few windows open to let the cool night air drift inside.

AJ peered inside the open window. "It looks like this must be the mom's bedroom." He started to climb through the window.

"Wait! What are you doing? You can't go in there!" I protested.

"Why not?" AJ answered, already halfway inside. "We're not going to find anything by standing in the yard!"

He was now inside, and apparently everyone else

saw things the way he did, because Traverna Lynn quickly jumped up and started climbing in right behind him. Scooter climbed in next. I reluctantly followed.

Once I had crawled inside and landed on the floor, I looked around. I could see what AJ was talking about. A small lamp on the nightstand shone, reflecting off a mirrored door, which led to the bedroom closet. The reflection made the room extra bright, especially after the darkness outside. There was a single dresser, the nightstand, and a large bed as the only pieces of furniture in the room. The quilt spread over the bed looked like something my grandma would have in her house. There were no pictures or other personal items lying around to indicate that anyone was even using this room. The only exception was a nursing uniform hanging on the back of the bedroom door. That door was halfway open, and Scooter was leaving through it. I scrambled to my feet so I could follow. I quickly walked to the door, careful not to touch anything, and quietly slipped into the darkness of the rest of the house.

CHAPTER 18
Trapped!

Once outside the bedroom, my eyes quickly adjusted, and I realized I was standing at the end of a hallway that went off to my left. To my right I could see the kitchen and living room. Light from the streetlight outside streamed through the spaces in the kitchen window's blinds, giving an eerie glow to the front rooms of the house. The living room had a couple couches, a television, and a treadmill. The house's front door had a little entryway, which sort of separated the kitchen from the living room. I heard a *psst* come from my left. I turned to see AJ at the other end of the hallway, outside what must have been Eddie's room, motioning for me to join him.

I moved as quickly as I could through the semi-darkness and joined AJ and the others in Eddie's room at the end of the hall. Eddie's room was the darkest yet. There was only one window, and the blinds were shut, so almost no light got in. Scooter had that taken care of. He had brought a couple flashlights in his backpack, and he and AJ each had one now. In order not to attract attention with the lights, both Scooter and AJ placed their hands over the faces of the flashlights so that only a little light would stream through their fingers.

With just that little light, I could see that the walls were covered with posters. I assumed they were for movies or more bands that I had never heard of. The bed was not made, and on his pillow was a phonebook, opened to the maps in the back. "Interesting," I said. I walked over to get a closer look. Scooter came over to offer some light from his flashlight. Traverna Lynn came over to check out what was worth breaking the silence over. Meanwhile, AJ continued to wander around looking for anything else interesting.

There was a large sheet of paper stuck in the crease of the phonebook. I picked up the piece of paper from the phonebook to get a better look. Scooter spread his fingers out a little more on the face of the flashlight to give us a little more light to read the note. As I looked at the note, I heard Scooter's surprised "Hmm!" and Traverna Lynn's gasp at the same time. The top of the note said:

Order must be maintained!

It was followed by two columns of Silverdale addresses. I quickly scanned the list and saw an address with Thackery Place on it. I whispered, "Hey, I think this is some sort of list of targets or something. Doesn't James live on Thackery Place? I think this is his address."

"Could be," Scooter answered. "If so, then Traverna Lynn's address would be on it too."

I held the piece of paper out for Traverna Lynn to see. She grabbed it out of my hand and scanned the list of about thirty addresses.

"Hey, guys, I think I got some good evidence over here!" It was AJ. He was over by the desk in the far corner of the room, and he was holding up some sort of spray can.

"What is it?" Scooter whispered.

"It's called Unlock-a-Lock, and it's supposed to help get rusty locks open."

"So what," Scooter said, disappointed. "He works at a bike shop; he probably has to get bike locks open all the time."

"I know, but listen to this warning." AJ started reading the back of the spray can: "Warning: Do not use padlock after applying Unlock-a-Lock. Chemicals in product are designed to release lock, but will compromise metal components in the process. If Unlock-a-Lock comes in contact with any unintended metal, wash with soap and water immediately. If left in contact with metal, the corrosive nature of Unlock-a-Lock could destroy metal in as little as five days."

He looked up from reading. "Remember how the brake lines looked like they had been dissolved by acid or something? This could be what di—"

Suddenly, a flash of light flowed from one side of the room to the other. The light had come from outside the window. The distinct roar of Eddie's car could now be heard in the driveway. *How did we not hear him coming a mile away?!* I guess we were too involved in our snooping to notice. AJ peeked through the blinds.

"Eddie's back already!" AJ dropped the can and sprinted from the room. Scooter followed. *Great, now both lights are gone!* Traverna Lynn shoved the list back into my hand. I fumbled in the dark, trying to put it back into the phonebook the way I'd found it. I heard the car door slam. Footsteps approached the front door. I stumbled out of the room. I blindly ran down the dark hall, toward the room we had entered from—toward freedom. But the hall also led closer to the front door, where Eddie was. *OOF!* I ran into Traverna Lynn just outside the mother's bedroom. I jerked her to her feet. I heard the key being shoved into the front door. There wasn't enough time for both of us to make it out of that window! I pushed her into the bedroom and turned around, sprinting back toward Eddie's room. I heard the front door open. I found Eddie's door. The kitchen light flicked on just as I ducked inside the bedroom.

I paused in the room, trying to think. *Think, Tyler, think! What to do now?* The additional light coming down the hall inspired me. *Window?* But there was no way I could get it open without the blinds making all kinds of noise. Eddie's footsteps sounded in the hall. I panicked (but don't tell AJ). I turned and saw Eddie's closet. It was a wide closet with two sliding doors, one in front of the other. Luckily, one side was open. A pile of clothes lay at the bottom of the open doorway. *No more thinking!* I jumped into the closet and ducked behind the other door. I stood as close as I could to the wall on the closed side.

Eddie turned the light on and stood in the doorway for a moment. *Please, please don't have a reason to get in your closet!* I thought. I looked over at the open side of the closet, where light poured in. I looked again at the pile of clothes on the floor. *Hmm, Eddie takes care of his dirty laundry the same way I do,* I said to myself. That thought triggered a more terrifying one: I realized I was standing in the middle of a bunch of hanging clothes. *Oh no! What if he needs a new shirt?* My heart was now pounding so loudly that I thought for sure that Eddie was going to find me in the closet just because of all the noise. I tried to slow my breathing and stay as still as possible as Eddie walked past the open closet door and went over to his bed. I started to panic again. *How long am I going to have to stay in here? What if he doesn't go to sleep right away? Is he a sound sleeper? Will I be able to get out of this closet, down the hall, and out of the window without waking him up?* If I had thought my heart was pounding before, now I felt like it was trying to escape from my ribcage. Over my thundering pulse, I could hear Eddie grab the piece of paper from the phonebook and mutter "Stupid!" under his breath. He quickly turned around and walked out of the room, shutting the light off as he went out.

I breathed a sigh of relief, but I didn't dare move. I could hear Eddie walk down the hall and rummage in the kitchen for a moment, and then that light went out as well. Eddie went out the front door. It closed, and I could hear it being locked. Then the car started up and backed out of the driveway. The night was so silent that I could still hear the car several blocks away. Even knowing the coast was clear, I didn't move for another minute. Finally, I inched my way out of the closet. I went over to the bed, looking at the phonebook to verify what I'd heard. The list of addresses was indeed gone. Eddie must have forgotten it and come back to get it before visiting the next address on the list.

I quickly moved down the hallway and into the bedroom. I had so much adrenaline rushing through me that I felt like I literally dove out the window into the grassy yard below. As soon as I hit the ground, AJ, Scooter, and Traverna Lynn came rushing out of the nearby bushes where they had been hiding. None of us said a word; we all just raced toward our bikes under the cover of the night.

CHAPTER 19
A-Hunting We Will Go

When we got back to the Birdcage, we decided we had had enough excitement in the dark for one night, so we said goodbye to Traverna Lynn and told her we would get a hold of her in the morning. Once we'd left her, the three of us boys still didn't do any talking on our way home. I think we just wanted to get to the safety of the Seeva home before we discussed all that had just happened.

It wasn't until we were in our sleeping bags on the floor of AJ's bedroom that AJ finally broke the silence. "Okay, so what happened in there, Ty? We thought you were right behind us! And when you weren't, I thought you were caught for sure!"

I tried to think of something sarcastic or witty to say, but nothing came to me at the moment. All I could manage to do was have my voice crack while I muttered, "Yee—um, yeah, me too."

I then cleared my throat and went on to explain that I'd had to spend time trying to get the list put back into the phonebook where I had found it, and by the time I tried to leave, it was too late. I told them how I had hidden in the closet while Eddie came into the room to retrieve the list, which seemed to be the only reason he had come back to the house in the first place.

"What do we do now?" AJ asked.

"I don't know," Scooter said. "It's obvious that Eddie is our bike vandal, but I don't know what we are going to do about it. I need some time to think!"

"Why do you say that? Didn't you see his hit list?" AJ prodded.

"No, when we were in the house, I was too busy looking at the addresses that had already been hit by the bike vandal. I didn't have time to memorize any of the addresses yet to be hit."

"So what you're saying is, we're back to where we started. Back to playing defense. I guess we wait for Eddie to make another move? But how is that going to help us?" I asked.

"But we know Eddie is the vandal! Let's just go to the police and Commander Coleman," AJ said.

"And tell them what?" I said. "The proof we have, we got from sneaking into Eddie's house! Do you want to explain that to the police?"

"Good point," AJ conceded.

"We do have the tracker info," I said. "We could tell them we suspected Eddie was the culprit and put a tracker on him—that is a true story. We could show him a printout of your recording of where the tracker has been; that should be enough for Commander Coleman to connect the dots and track down Eddie himself. And at that point he should be able to find the evidence—the evidence we know is out there—his own way."

"Yeah, that might work," said Scooter. "Right now, though, I don't have any printout that ties the tracker to any reported crimes from the newspaper or from The Network. It's weird—The Network has been pretty quiet recently regarding our request for any info about broken or stolen bikes. But I'll go check it in the morning. We should be able to see where Eddie went overnight. Hopefully, we will also hear about another broken bicycle, and we can tie the two to the same location.

"Okay, sounds like a plan," I said.

Apparently that was the end of the conversation because the next thing I knew, I got a pillow smacked in my face. We quickly put our thoughts about the case aside; AJ had started a pillow fight, and we each set our mind on being the one to finish it.

I am not sure what time we finally went to sleep. Between all the pillow fights, pranks that never get old, and late-night jokes, I lost track of the time. It must have been pretty late, though, because all three of us slept in until almost 10 a.m. Scooter was already awake when I woke up, his hands behind his head on his pillow. I could see he was deep in thought as he stared blankly at the ceiling. Luckily, I was the second one to wake up. I say "luckily," because I think it's an unwritten rule that whoever is the last to wake up is supposed to get dogpiled by everyone who is awake. And who are we to argue with such a rule? AJ was still sound asleep, his sleeping bag pulled over his head to keep out the morning light. I quietly tapped Scooter on the elbow and motioned toward the sleeping AJ. He knew what I was thinking, and without either of us saying a word, we both jumped onto AJ. Even half asleep, he was almost able to buck both of us off of him, but his sleeping-bag prison proved to be too hard for him to escape. He eventually resorted to whining until we finally got off of him and let him out of his little fluffy cocoon.

I usually don't do very well when I don't start my day with a shower. But we were all pretty excited to dive back into the case, and so I had to get over it. We quickly cleaned up AJ's room by stuffing all of the sleeping bags and our extra clothes under his bed. Then we rushed downstairs to grab a quick breakfast before heading over to HQ. There was no milk in the fridge for cereal, but there was a bunch of bananas in a bowl on the counter and half of a leftover pizza from a couple nights earlier. Scooter is not a fan of leftover pizza (cold or reheated), which is fine by me; that leaves more for the rest of us. AJ and I split it between us and each wolfed down two pieces cold.

As we went outside and started walking through the woods toward HQ, Scooter spoke up. "What do you think the paper meant when it said, 'Order must be maintained'?" That must have been what Scooter was thinking about as he stared at the ceiling that morning.

"I think Eddie was supposed to break the bikes in the order they were put on the list," I said.

"Why would that matter?" AJ asked.

"Good question," Scooter agreed. "It doesn't seem like the order in which you break the bikes would matter very much."

"That's why the list said the order must be maintained," I argued. "Otherwise, if the paper were truly a target list, then Eddie would do what was most convenient. He'd do the list in order from easiest to hardest or from nearest to farthest or something logical like that."

"If order were important, then that little reminder would make sense. But I am arguing that I don't see why order is important," Scooter explained.

"Yeah, I don't know *why* it's important, but it is," I continued. "'Order must be maintained.' I think if we figure out why the order is so important, then this case will finish solving itself."

"Maybe it means a different kind of order," AJ jumped in. "Not order like A, then B, then C, but actually *order*—like the opposite of chaos. So 'Order must be maintained' is saying, 'Don't let things turn to chaos.'"

Scooter and I both laughed. "So how is breaking bikes going to help maintain order?" Scooter teased.

"Um, well, maybe those people were threatening the establishment, and Eddie is a hired gun to get them back in line!"

"That is the most ridiculous thing I have ever heard," I countered. "AJ, I think you've been watching too many conspiracy movies!"

"They said you would say that," AJ joked, poking fun at himself as we reached the hidden blackberry door at the end of the Straight-a-Way tunnel. The conversation ended there as we all got quiet so we could enter HQ in silent secrecy.

Once inside the shelter, AJ made a beeline for the fridge while Scooter immediately got on the computer. I laid down on the couch and just stared up at our map on the wall next to me. I don't know why I was staring at the map. From my angle, I couldn't really see anything. It reminded me of going to the movies and being stuck at the side of the very front row. Sitting there, I could never get a good look at any of the action sequences, and I would leave the theater with the biggest kink in my neck.

Scooter let out a loud "Oh shoot!" that pulled me away from my memories and back to the case at hand.

"What's up, Scoot?" AJ said as he walked up behind Scooter. He had found an apple and was chomping away.

"Look here! It appears that right now, Eddie is just up the road from us—in Spirit Ridge."

"That's great!" AJ said, excited. "Let's go try and catch him in the act!"

"Oh, wait. It looks like there's a problem. It looks like he has been there since about 1 a.m. I'm guessing he is not actually there. It's more likely that the tracker finally came off of his backpack," Scooter said with disappointment.

"There is only one way to find out: let's go!" AJ headed toward the shelter door.

"Okay, but this could be like finding a needle in a haystack," I said. "Scooter, didn't you say the tracking software only narrows the location down to an intersection? Those trackers are pretty small."

"That's true, Ty," Scooter replied. "That is still a large area to narrow down where the tracker may have fallen off, and I would like to get it back if possible." He then put on his thinking face and let out a loud "Hmm" at the same time.

"Well let's just go," AJ suggested. "Maybe we'll get lucky and find it lying out in the open or something. At least we'll be able to see who lives in that area. We can see if anyone heard or saw anything unusual last night."

"I've got it!" Scooter exclaimed, snapping out of his intense thoughts. "We can go Rabbit Hunting!"

"What?" AJ and I both asked in unison.

"That is so random! Why would you be thinking of hunting rabbits right now?" I added. "I thought you were thinking about how to find that tracker and solve this case."

"I was, actually," Scooter said. "We will find the tracker by doing some good old Rabbit Hunting."

Scooter then went on to explain that his dad used to play a game called Rabbit Hunting when he was a teenager. One of Mr. Parks' friends would go hide somewhere in the neighborhood with a walkie-talkie and then start talking into it. The other kids would take the other walkie-talkie. They would not just listen to what the hiding kid was saying; they would look at how strong the walkie-talkie's signal was. The signal was measured by a series of red lights on the handset. If all the red lights were lit up, then the signal was strong, and that meant they were close to the friend who was hiding. If the signal was weak, then only a couple of red lights would light up, and they would know they were far away from the hiding friend. I'm sure you already figured out that the friend that was hiding was the Rabbit and the other friends were the Hunters.

"I think we can use a similar concept to find our lost tracker," Scooter continued. "The tracker is transmitting a signal that my computer is picking up—that's how we know the general location of the tracker. My dad has a device in the garage for measuring the amount of 'unwanted frequencies' a computer gives off when it's running. I think I can modify it a little bit so that it will measure the signal strength of our tracker."

"Uh, we'll take your word for it," I said.

"Okay then. Why don't you guys stay here. I'm

going to go to my garage; it shouldn't take too long." He hustled out the door.

AJ and I were pretty sure he was going to be wrong about how long it was going to take, so we immediately came up with a way to pass the time. We decided to have a little shooting contest. A while ago, AJ had brought to HQ a little dart gun that shot six suction-cup darts. He used it to distract and annoy Scooter any chance he got. Well, now we were going to use it to have a shooting contest. We quickly made some small paper targets from the printer paper and placed them at different points around the sink, assigning them each different point values based on how large they were and how far away they were from the shooter. Then we took turns sitting on the futon and seeing who could score the most points with the six bullets.

As expected, Scooter took a long time and didn't show up until we had each had five turns. At that point, I had four wins and AJ only had one. Oh yeah! Take that, AJ!

Unfortunately, AJ was too busy laughing for my taunting to be effective. He was laughing at Scooter, who had shown up holding the craziest-looking contraption. It was the size of a deck of cards, but then it had a wand sticking out of one side, with a metal coat hanger wrapped around the wand over and over again, sort of in the shape of a tornado.

"What's with the coat hanger?" AJ asked, still laughing.

"Well, normally you wave this wand near the computer to search for frequencies, but I need the device to be searching outside for a signal. So I wrapped this coat hanger around the wand to act as an antenna and pick up the signal better."

"Well, okay, whatever works!" I laughed.

"Let's go already!" AJ said impatiently and headed for the door. Scooter and I followed, closing the large vault door behind us. Then we climbed the ladder to the blackberry bushes and daylight.

We squat-walked out of the bushes using the Straight-a-Way and then walked through the woods back toward the house. When we reached the lawn, Mrs. Parks opened the back door and stepped out onto the back porch.

"Sean, I need you to watch your brother for a couple of hours. I have a meeting with the hostess committee, and they don't allow children to attend." Urpy walked out the door and wrapped his arms around his mom's right leg. He seemed rather mellow this morning.

"But, Mom, we were about to go track down a lead for this case we're working on!" Scooter argued.

"Then take him with you," she insisted.

"But, Mom, it might be da—" He caught himself mid-thought, but it was too late.

"Dangerous? Sean, if whatever you are doing is too risky to take Wyatt with you, then you should not be doing it, either!"

"No, it's not like that. It just makes things harder,

that's all."

This is why I do most of the talking, I said to myself.

Mrs. Parks smiled. "You boys are very smart. I am sure you will find a way to accomplish what you need to with your little brother along. In fact, I bet you can do it even better!" With that, she pried Urpy off of her leg, walked back inside the house, and shut the back door. With nothing—or rather no one—to hold onto, Urpy quickly jumped off the back porch, ran over, and began hugging his big brother.

Good, little Urpy. Fun kid, full of energy. And he adored "Ooter." That's the best he could manage at saying Scooter's name. And Mrs. Parks would turn out to have been right. I think things just might have gone better because Urpy came with us. I will let you be the judge.

CHAPTER 20
Lost and Found

We ended up walking, since Urpy did not have a bicycle with which he could keep up with us. Plus, Scooter had to carry around his funny-looking Dip-O-Meter, which might be hard to carry while riding a bike. It's not really called a Dip-O-Meter, but I can neither pronounce nor spell what Scooter called it, so I am sticking with the nickname.

We didn't have to walk that far to get to the intersection where we knew the tracker was located. The intersection was actually a *T*, and we looked around to try and guess what Eddie might have been doing at this location. We were standing in the middle of the main road (the top bar of the *T*), Ridgeline Drive. To our left was a long, tall wooden fence, similar to the one that surrounds AJ's house. The same fence ran along the backyards of several houses. I guessed you actually accessed the front of these houses by going down another street in the neighborhood. To our right was a street called Parkview Road. It came down a hill, ran into Ridgeline Drive, and dead-ended; the fenced yards were across the intersection from it. Parkview was actually one of the entrances into the Spirit Ridge housing development. At the top of the hill, it connected to the main road into town, Silverdale Way. Parkview was a pretty short road. On each corner of the intersection on the Parkview side, there was a house. That meant we had five possibilities as to which house was Eddie's target the night before: the two houses to our right, on each side of Parkview, and the three houses to our left that we couldn't really see because of the tall fence guarding their backyards.

"Okay," Scooter began, "let's hope there are no other things in the neighborhood putting out a signal that would throw off our Rabbit Hunting." He turned on the Dip-O-Meter. It made a little *boop*, and then the little needle started moving wildly between the numbers 0 and 14, eventually settling on the number 9. The *boop* from the Dip-O-Meter had gotten the attention of Urpy, and now he insisted on holding it.

"Okay, Wyatt, you can hold it, but you have to be careful and not drop it. And you have to walk where I tell you," Scooter instructed his little brother. He turned to us. "We must already be close if the frequency reading is at 9. You guys look around, and let's walk along the fence line for starters."

We walked a few feet to our left toward the fence. There was a small strip of grass between the fence and the asphalt road. We started to move straight ahead along the fence line. AJ and I scanned the grass next to the fence while Scooter looked over Urpy's shoulder and called out what the Dip-O-Meter was showing.

"Still at 9," he declared. We heard a car approaching. I turned around to see a police car coming down Parkview Road from the neighborhood entrance. I froze. I was pretty sure we weren't doing anything wrong, but that didn't stop my heart from beating twice as fast as it was a second ago. The police car slowed to make the turn, and when the driver saw Urpy, he broke into a smile. He gave a slight wave of his hand and drove away. I sighed in relief.

We continued down the fence line, and then Scooter said, "Uh-oh, we are now at 8. I think we need to go the other direction." So we turned around and started walking back the other way along the fence. Pretty soon Scooter said, "Okay, we are back at 9... Now it's 10... Now 11! We must be on the right track. 12!" AJ and I were getting excited, searching more frantically, each wanting to be the one to spot the tracker first. "Okay, we are now at 13. That's almost full strength. It must be right around here someplace."

We continued to search for a few more seconds before AJ exclaimed, "I think I got it!" He reached into the grass right up against the fence. He held up the little device, which was about the size of a quarter. "Is this it?"

"Sure is," Scooter said as he took it out of AJ's open hand. "And it looks like it hasn't been damaged. That's good. That means Eddie probably didn't find it; it must have just fallen off his backpack."

"So then the question is, what was Eddie doing in this spot? Do you think he was trying to hop the fence right here to get into this backyard?" I asked, pointing to the house we could see rising above the fence line. "Do you think he succeeded in getting over the fence and breaking something?"

"Well, maybe we should simply walk around to the front and ask," Scooter suggested.

"Sounds good," AJ agreed. We started heading back down Ridgeline Drive, looking for a connecting street leading to the house.

I decided that whoever designed this stupid neighborhood had actually let their three-year-old draw some scribbled lines on a piece of paper; they had called those roads, and then they had just put houses in wherever they could fit them. I say this because it was a really long and indirect route to get to the front of the house that we were just looking at from behind.

I'm sure by car it would not have been that bad, but when you have to walk and you just want some answers, it seems like a really long way. Anyway, as we finally came around the corner and could see the front driveway of the house that we were talking about, we saw there was a police car in the driveway. I assumed it was the same car we had seen a few minutes earlier.

"I guess that answers our question about whether anything happened at that house or not," Scooter observed.

Just then the police officer walked out the front door of the house, headed toward his car. He turned our way and saw us. The three of us older boys turned around and acted like we hadn't seen him. Scooter had to physically turn Urpy around by the shoulders and nudge him to start walking the way we had just come. The officer yelled, but we tried to keep walking as if we hadn't heard. We foolishly tried to speed up. Just then, another police car came around the corner in front of us. *Great. Now we're stuck.* We all looked at each other as the new police cruiser drove right toward us and then came to a stop in front of us. The sun created a glare on the windshield, which prevented us from seeing who was inside—or more importantly, what sort of mood that person happened to be in.

That mystery was quickly solved: the door opened, and out stepped Commander Coleman! The fact that I could see him clenching his teeth through a fake smile told me that he was not happy. He pointed at the ground, which we took as a clear command for us to sit as he began to speak.

"So, this morning we have a report of another trespassing and vandalism last night. So I send Officer Evans to check it out. And who does he see but three teenagers and a toddler out for a walk?

Strange? Yes. Suspicious? Maybe. But he goes and does his job of getting a statement from the property owner. But then he overhears those same teenagers discussing the very crime he came to investigate. Naturally, Officer Evans wonders why these teenagers know more about the crime than he does. So he calls me, and right away I know what three teenage boys he's talking about." With that last statement, he gave each of us a personalized glare.

AJ turned to give me a look of complete confusion. I was trying to put the pieces together myself. The officer must have been in the backyard at the time and heard us discussing the case just on the other side of the fence. Oops.

Commander Coleman went on. "So tell me, gentlemen. Is it coincidence that there was another late-night trespass and you three happen to show up in the morning?"

I think all three of us knew better than to answer with a yes. Scooter slowly spoke as he bowed his head, "No, sir."

"Then my next question is, how? How did you hear about this? We haven't even created a police report yet."

It was time to come clean. Sort of. I began to explain to Commander Coleman how we suspected Eddie, based on the fact that he was at both bike races, the fact that he worked at a bike shop so he might have had a way to profit from the vandalisms, and the fact that in general, he just gave off a "creepy" vibe. That was enough for us to begin tracking his movements with Scooter's homemade tracking device. All of that was the truth, although I left out the part about Eddie's house and the list. I then told him that our tracking software showed that Eddie had permanently stopped at this location, so we came to see what had happened. That's when we'd found that the tracker was here and Eddie was not.

"So now we can't follow Eddie anymore because we don't have a way of tracking him, unless we can run into him again and re-apply the tracker," I concluded.

Commander Coleman listened intently until I was finished with the whole story. But AJ chimed in before Coleman could respond. "We would have come to you sooner, but we just now were able to verify that there was a crime in the first place. You would have been our next call."

"Oh, I'm sure," Coleman said with a laugh and a roll of his eyes.

"So now you can go and arrest Eddie," AJ pleaded. "He's probably down at the bike shop, working as we speak."

"It's not quite that simple, AJ. We don't have any proof of anything. And although your little tracker might have you convinced that this Eddie fella is your guy, we police have to base our investigation on more solid facts. Unfortunately, we have to practically catch the bad guys in the act in order to send them to jail. It's sad, really. I don't suppose you have any brilliant ideas on how to do that, do you?"

"Catching him in the act?" I jumped in. "That was our goal, but no, we don't."

Commander Coleman bent over and fussed with Urpy's hair, "Well, then you should leave the rest of this investigation to us. You just worry about watching this little guy." He stood up and headed back to his car. He stood in the doorway, leaning over the open door, staring at us as if he were waiting for something.

Finally, Scooter said, "Oh, right, I guess we should be going, then." He stood up to walk back home. AJ and I were right behind him. This pleased Coleman, and he smiled as he climbed back into his car. As we walked down the street and around the corner, we could see him drive over to the other police car to talk to Officer Evans.

"Well, back to playing defense, I'm afraid," Scooter said as we slowly walked back to the Parks' house.

CHAPTER 21
One Last Chance

As we neared Scooter's house, we could see that Traverna Lynn was sitting on the front walkway, waiting for us. She had her knees pulled up to her chest and her arms wrapped around them to help her keep her balance. Her chin was resting on her knees, and she looked like she could fall asleep that way. But then she jumped up to her feet the second she saw us. It was then that I realized we had forgotten to call her in the morning. Poor girl, I'm sure she had a ton of questions. She wasn't able to debrief what had happened the night before, the way that we did.

"I thought you were going to call," she said, sounding more confused than angry.

"I'm sorry; we forgot. A lot happened this morning," Scooter said apologetically.

"Oh, that's okay. I'm already over it," Traverna Lynn said, "But I want you to know, I would have called you if the tables were reversed."

"I am sure you would," Scooter laughed. "Come on, let's go inside, and I'll fill you in over lunch."

When we got inside, Scooter began rummaging through the kitchen for lunch, but he was soon interrupted when Mrs. Parks got home from her committee thingy. She brought home a whole plate full of little sandwiches with the crusts removed, and we each managed to find a kind that we liked. Combine that with a gallon of milk from the fridge, and lunch was served. Mrs. P had eaten more sandwiches than she needed while at her committee meeting, so she excused herself and went into the other room to fold laundry. Scooter then filled Traverna Lynn in on what had happened to Eddie's tracker, as well as the conversation we'd just had with Commander Coleman.

"So what it all boils up to is, we're back to where we started!" Traverna Lynn said as he finished his story.

"Pretty much," he answered, and then he lowered his voice so he wouldn't be heard by Mrs. P in the next room. "And the worst part is, we can't tell the police how we know so much. Unless we want to tell them we broke into Eddie's house."

She replied, "Maybe we should tell the police everything, and let the chips fall in May."

AJ chuckled and then whispered, "Yeah, and we would all be grounded until high school!"

"Actually, that wouldn't really help much, anyway," Scooter said matter-of-factly. "Other than the fact that we know there is a target list with some addresses on it, they know as much as we do now."

"Man, if we only had a copy of that list!" I whispered. "At least then we could get out ahead of Eddie and set a trap for the next address!"

"You should have just held onto it, Ty," AJ whispered.

"Yeah, then we would have been caught for sure!" I said defensively. "As it was, I had to improvise because you ran out of the room with the flashlight!"

AJ snapped back, "I left Scooter there to help you!"

"More like you abandoned all of us as you ran to safety," Scooter said.

"Well, you guys took too long looking at that stupid list. You were the ones who put us in danger," AJ argued.

I jumped in, trying to bring the conversation back down to a whisper, "What put us in danger was you going into the house in the first place!"

"You weren't even that helpful once we got inside, anyway!" Scooter said, poking his finger in AJ's chest.

AJ stood up to remind Scooter that he was bigger. Scooter stood up to show AJ he was not afraid. I stood up to have a better chance of getting a word in.

Meanwhile, Traverna Lynn just sat there, chomping away at her tuna sandwich, watching the three of us argue while trying to whisper so as not to be heard by Mrs. Parks in the next room. This went on for a little longer until Scooter finally stopped arguing and just calmly sat down. That sort of took the fun out of the fight, and AJ and I sat back down as well.

Scooter turned to me and stared directly into my eyes as if he thought he might find the answer to his next question there. "Tyler, can you remember anything else from the list. Anything that might help us?"

"No, nothing I haven't already told you guys," I answered, frustrated that I couldn't help. "It's not like I have a photographic memory like Trav—" All three of us stared at each other for a second, blinked, and slowly turned to look at Traverna Lynn.

"Wha?" she said, her mouth half full of sandwich.

"Traverna Lynn, you got a look at the list, right? Do you remember what's on it?" Scooter asked rather excitedly.

"Of course. What do you want to know?" she said calmly.

"Anything. Everything. How much of it do you remember?" AJ chimed in.

"All of it."

AJ was hysterical. "We've been fighting over nothing for the last five minutes, and you just sat there? Why didn't you say something earlier?"

"You never asked me."

AJ slapped his forehead and exhaled loudly, a mix of elation and frustration escaping his body.

"Well, let me get some paper, and let's reproduce this list!" Scooter said, getting up from the table.

"Let's head up to my room, where I should have some blank printer paper."

We all scrambled upstairs to Scooter's room. AJ and I plopped down on the bed and Traverna Lynn stood. Scooter grabbed some paper and handed it to me to write down what Traverna Lynn was about to recite to us.

"Okay," she began, "at the top of the page, it said, 'Order must be maintained.'"

Scooter interrupted her. "I still think that's the key. I think if we figure out what that means, we will know the *why*. I think we pretty much know the *who, what, when, where,* and *how.*"

"Does it matter right now?" AJ asked, wanting to get on with it.

"It does to me," Scooter answered. "Plus, if order must be maintained, then Eddie probably hit these addresses in order. So I'm going to plot the addresses in sequence, using a mapping program on my computer. Then I can compare it later to the map of reported crimes from The Network." Obviously, we would have to do that later, when Traverna Lynn wasn't around and we could get down to HQ.

Scooter went over to the computer sitting on his desk and turned on the monitor. Of course, this was actually just a screen that was looking at his supercomputer in HQ, but to the casual observer, it looked like an ordinary desktop computer.

Traverna Lynn proceeded to rattle off the addresses from the list, while I wrote them on the paper and

Scooter typed them into the computer to be mapped out. When it was finished, Scooter saved the list and the map to his computer so we could later compare things to the map on the wall in HQ. I asked him if he would also email them to me so I would have them for our records, and he did. The four of us then huddled around the list I had just finished writing.

I'm not sure what the others were looking for, but my eyes went straight to the end of the list. I noticed while we were walking earlier that day that the house that had been the target last night faced Sol Duc Street. I wanted to know how many address-es came after a Sol Duc Street address—that would tell us how many more targets Eddie had left to do. It didn't take but a second to see that 5936 Sol Duc Street was the second to last address on the list.

"Uh, guys, we may have a problem." I pointed at the penultimate address. "This Sol Duc address is where we were this morning."

"That means Eddie only has one more house to hit!" AJ exclaimed.

"And how much do you want to bet, he goes after it tonight?" Scooter added. He stood up and headed for the door.

"Where are you headed?" I asked.

"We had better check out that last address, see what we have to work with. I recognize Silverhill Place. It's pretty close to us—just off Gallery Street—so let's go."

"Wait, wait, wait! What do you mean 'see what we

have to work with? What are you thinking?" I asked.

"I'm thinking this could be our last chance to catch this guy in the act. So that's what I plan on doing."

"And how do you propose we do that?" I asked, skeptical.

"I don't know. That's why I have to go see the house, see where they keep the bike I presume Eddie will be after, see how easy it would be to catch or corner Eddie—you know, stuff like that."

"Why don't we just tell the police we have a hunch that Eddie is going to go to that address tonight and have them stake out the house?" I asked.

"Oh, come on, you know they won't go for that, Ty," he countered.

"Well, what are you going to say if we catch Eddie and then the police want to know how we knew he would be at that address?"

"I don't know. That's your job," Scooter said as he smiled and patted my shoulder. "Besides, we are just going to check it out. There might not even be an opportunity to catch him at this house. That's why we *have* to go check it out. Come on." He walked out of the room without even turning back to see if we were following.

Traverna Lynn laughed. "Well, Tyler, looks like you are stuck between a rock and the grindstone," she said as she walked out of the room. AJ was right behind her, and once again, I reluctantly followed, turning out the light as I left the bedroom.

CHAPTER 22

Work with What You've Got

The bike ride to the last address was quick and uneventful. We stopped a few houses away and surveyed the neighborhood.

Scooter spoke first. "So be on the lookout for Eddie's car; you should be able to hear it coming. If we have to come during the day to check things out, I am sure Eddie will want to do the same. He could show up at any minute."

"Wouldn't Eddie be at work?" Traverna Lynn asked.

"Oh, good point," Scooter answered. "Yeah, he probably would be. Well then, let's take a look and get out of here before Eddie gets off work and has a chance to get here."

We set our bikes just inside some nearby bushes on an undeveloped lot and headed toward the houses on foot. The plan was to walk right past the house at first and see what we could at a quick glance and then figure out our next move after that.

The target house was a two-story yellow house with probably the nicest front lawn of any house in the neighborhood. Come to think of it, the house looked a lot like Scooter's house. The driveway was on the left side, which ran up to a garage. There was some sort of room above the garage with a window overlooking the street. As we got closer, I could see there was a privacy fence between the yellow house and the neighboring house to the left, which we were currently walking in front of. The fence took a turn and ran right up to the side of the house. Since the fence was over six feet tall, we really couldn't see much of what might be behind it. As we walked past the driveway, we could see a couple of newspapers piled up on the front step.

"Those newspapers are good news. It looks like the owner of the house has been gone a couple of days," Scooter observed. "I am sure Eddie will find that convenient too."

We kept walking past the house, and on the right side, we could see more of the same type of fence as on the left side. But the right side had an iron gate that allowed us to see part of the backyard. We kept walking all the way down to the end of the block, at which point Scooter spoke up again.

"Since the owners of the house appear to be gone, it looks like we might be able to set a trap in the backyard. I noticed by looking through the gate that there was no fence along the back of the yard—just the tree line. So let's go into the woods right here and work our way back to the yellow house that way."

He tried jumping into the bushes we were standing next to, but the bushes were too thick and he bounced back onto the sidewalk. He gave a dejected look, and then he looked at AJ and pointed at the spot in the bushes he had just tried to plow through. AJ proudly used his bigger size to start blazing a trail for the rest of us to follow. We worked our way single-file behind AJ as he clawed his way deeper into the woods. Once we got past the first wave of thick bushes, it actually got pretty easy to move around. The tall, mature trees were so big that they kept most of the sunlight out, which meant not as much undergrowth could survive. We went back deep enough that we would be behind all the houses and their backyards, and then we started working our way back toward our target house.

While we walked, every once in a while, we would catch a flash of color from a glimpse of the house we were walking behind. That's how we knew we had arrived behind the right house. A two-story yellow house tends to stick out, even when you're under the canopy of some big trees. As we approached the backyard, once again the going got tough as the bushes started to get really thick. After what seemed way too long, we arrived at the back edge of the backyard.

We were surprised to find the backyard was almost completely covered in dirt. There were tiny grass sprouts everywhere. That's when I realized that the homeowners must have just recently planted grass in the backyard. It looked bad right now, but after a few weeks of sunshine and a little Washington rain, they would probably have a back lawn that looked just as good as the front.

Near the back porch was a giant hammock that must have been built for holding two or three people at once. It was held up by a stand-alone frame of metal triangles, so it didn't need a tree or anything like that. On the back porch were a huge barbeque grill and a plastic sandbox. The sandbox made me laugh—after all, right now they already had a huge sandbox: it was called the backyard! I knew eventually that would no longer be the case, but it still made me chuckle. Then I found something else to chuckle at: there was a lawnmower on the side of the house without the gate. On the opposite side of the house (the side with the gate) there were a couple of trash cans. From across the yard, we could see that there was no bicycle in the backyard. Uh-oh, that's bad news. What if the bicycle were locked away in the garage? Eddie wouldn't break into the garage in order to finish the list, would he?

AJ noticed the same thing I had: "I don't see a bike. What do you think that means?"

"It means the owners might have taken it with them when they left town," Scooter said as he stepped into the backyard. "Come on, let's take a closer look."

"But what if there's no bike to vandalize?" AJ asked.

"Oh, there will be one. We might have to use one of ours as bait." Scooter continued walking toward the house. We reluctantly followed.

When we got to the back porch, we came across some good news. Leaning up against the house, near the far end of the porch, was an old ten-speed bicycle, the kind with the curvy handle bars. We couldn't see it from our spot across the yard because it was completely shielded by the large barbeque grill. We all sighed in relief. I don't think any of us were really looking forward to our bicycle being destroyed by Eddie—even for the sake of catching him.

"Well, there we go," Scooter said. "We have our bicycle for bait!"

"So what's the plan?" AJ said, rubbing his hands together in excited anticipation.

"Well, we have to catch Eddie with some incriminating evidence, either catch him with the list in his pocket, or better yet, catch him with that backpack full of tools that the police can match to some of the previous bicycle damage."

"Yeah, but how," AJ questioned.

"I am not sure," Scooter said. "I am trying to think of what equipment I have at home that would not be too much trouble for us to haul over here."

"Hold up, Scoot," I interrupted. "We can't really use any stuff from home."

"Why not?" Scooter asked.

"Well, you told me to figure out what to say once

we catch Eddie. The police are going to want to know why we're here."

"Yeah, so?"

"Well, I'm going to tell them we followed Eddie here."

"That sounds as good as anything," he said.

"Yeah, well, that means we have to act like we just got here. If we have a whole bunch of gadgets that we brought from home, that's going to contradict our story."

"Fine, we'll use what we have here." Scooter paused for a second and then went over to the hammock. "Aidge, come over here and help me untie this thing."

"Wait, I thought we were just going to scope things out right now. What are you doing?" Traverna Lynn asked, confused.

"If Eddie comes here during the daylight and sees the hammock, and then at night the hammock is gone, he is going to be suspicious," Scooter explained. He had his end detached from one side of the frame and motioned for AJ to do the same with his end.

"Oh, so the hammock is part of the plan?" Traverna Lynn asked. "How is that going to work?" She looked over at AJ, who had gotten his end untied and was now trying to pick up all the webbing of the hammock. He had managed to get himself tangled up in the webbing and was having a hard time working his way free. "Oh, I see, never mind!" She laughed out loud as all of us worked together to free AJ.

Scooter then took the ten-speed bike and set it down on the ground, leaning against the raised porch. He grabbed the hammock webbing and set it behind the barbeque. Then he looked at the arrangement of items and nodded. "Let's go," he said as he started heading back across the dirt backyard toward the woods we came from.

On the way home, Scooter explained the plan.

Since the barbeque grill was so big, AJ and I would hide behind it with the hammock at the ready. Scooter would be in the bushes across the yard with one of his uber-bright flashlights that we use when we go camping. When Eddie came into the backyard, he would see the bike and go over and work on damaging it in some way. While he wasn't ·looking, AJ and I would sneak out from behind the grill, throw the hammock net on him, and wrap him up. If we needed help getting Eddie to look the other way, Scooter could make some noise from the bushes or blind him with the large flashlight.

Meanwhile, Traverna Lynn would be the look-out from the street. Scooter would give her a little whistle from Urpy's "annoying toys" collection, and if she saw some something from the front of the house that would put us in more danger than we anticipated, then she was to blow the whistle with three short blasts, at which point we in the backyard would abandon the mission. Also, once we got started, if she sensed things were not going as planned and we needed help, she could blow that whistle like crazy and alert the neighbors. Assuming things did go according to plan, Traverna Lynn would then blow her whistle and then ask the first neighbor to come outside if she could borrow their phone to call the police. Then they would come to come pick up Eddie, along with his backpack and all the evidence tying him to all the vandalisms.

So once we got to Scooter's house, we all parted ways for the afternoon. We agreed to meet at AJ's house at 8 p.m. That would be enough time to get over to the last house on Eddie's list and into our places by 9 p.m. It would start getting dark by then, and Eddie could be coming anytime after that. Hopefully, it would be sooner, rather than later. If he waited until 1 a.m., like he had for some of the other crimes, then I wasn't sure I would be able to sit still in my hiding place that long.

CHAPTER 23

Make Sure to
Wash Behind the Ears

The rest of the afternoon was painfully long. I tried to distract myself from the anticipation by being as helpful around the house as possible. I helped my mom set the table for dinner and helped with some of the meal prep as well. She was grateful—and suspicious. At dinner I asked if I could spend the night at AJ's house again. She reminded me that I had just spent the night before over there as well. Early on in the conversation, I could tell she was going to say yes, but she was going to make me work for it. I begged her and even threw in the "Hey, it's summertime" argument. Eventually she got around to saying "Fine," which I'm pretty sure is what she was going to say from the beginning.

It's one thing for Scooter and me to get permission to spend the night at AJ's house. But I thought it would be a completely different story for Traverna Lynn to be away from her house after dark. I was worried she wasn't going to be able to figure out a way to stay out as late as our plan may require. She assured us it would not be a problem and that she would be at AJ's house at eight, but I still had my doubts.

Meanwhile, I looked for my black gloves, which I had forgotten the night before, but I never could find them. I wasted too much time on my search, so by the time I rode my bicycle into AJ's driveway, it was a little after 8 p.m. AJ and Scooter were waiting on the front steps. Traverna Lynn was nowhere to be seen. *Great. Just as I thought.* Now we would have to change the plan up a bit. Scooter began to lecture me about being on time, but I ignored him and walked past him up the stairs so I could go get changed. As soon as I did that, we could get on the road. As I reached for the door handle, the door opened, and there stood Traverna Lynn. Apparently, she had needed to use the bathroom and felt she had time since I was running late. Now Scooter's harassment about my tardiness made more sense! I was a little embarrassed. It's pretty bad if the girl who lives over a mile down the hill can get to AJ's house on time, but I who live only two houses away can't!

Apparently, I was worried for no reason. Traverna Lynn's parents were out for the evening, and Arwen was left in charge. Traverna Lynn said her sister would cover for her if their parents got back before she did.

Anyway, let's move on to the nightmare that the rest of the night was about to become. As planned, we rode up to the neighborhood we had been at earlier in the day and ditched our bikes in the bushes near where we had entered earlier. Traverna Lynn left us to go find a good hiding spot somewhere around the front of the house. The three of us boys worked our way through the woods back to the target house. We tried to use as little light from the flashlight as we could, in order not to attract any attention. When we got to the backyard of the yellow house, Scooter found a comfy spot in the bushes at the edge of the woods while AJ and I headed for the barbeque on the back porch.

I am not sure if it was good luck or bad, but something rare happened that particular night—at least rare for Washington—there was not a cloud in the sky. The moon was just shy of being full and was so bright that AJ and I could easily see the whole backyard. That meant getting to our hiding spot was really easy. We began to walk across the backyard toward the back porch. I hadn't noticed earlier in the day because we'd had so much else to think about, but the dirt seemed very soft under our feet. In an effort to save an old bike, I hoped we weren't ruining the newly planted lawn.

AJ and I got to the barbeque and crouched behind it. We found the hammock right where Scooter had tossed it. We unrolled and untangled it as best we could without actually leaving our hiding place. We eventually found the two ends of the hammock and each took one. I peeked around the corner of the barbeque. The bicycle was still sitting there, only five feet away. I figured as long as Eddie put his head down for a just a couple seconds while he messed with that bike, AJ and I should be able to spring from our hiding spot and toss the hammock on top of him before he even realized what was going on. Once the net was on top of him, then we could each hold our end of the hammock and spin around him a couple times, and Eddie would be wrapped up tight like a cocoon.

I imagined it was probably about 9:15 by the time AJ and I were all set. We both settled in for what we figured would be a long wait.

I began to think about the case. This was only our second major case, but it had turned into a strange one. *I mean, a hit list of bicycles to destroy? Really? It doesn't get any odder than that. Wait, "odder"? Is that even a word? Or is it "more odd"? I mean, "odder" just sounds odd, doesn't it? I'm pretty sure that can't be right.*

My argument with myself was interrupted by the approaching roar of an engine. I'm not one of those crazy guys who can recognize a car by the way it sounds, but I just knew that roar had to be from Eddie's car. The engine roar turned into a low rumble as the car slowed down in the neighborhood. I could tell the car was somewhere near the house we were hiding behind when the engine idled and then stopped. AJ and I both sat up straight; we were now on high alert.

I can see now why Eddie had yet to be caught even though he had broken so many bicycles. It was dead silent for a few minutes until I heard the faint sound of the bicycle softly scraping against the back porch. We hadn't even heard him sneak into the yard! I peeked cautiously around the corner of the barbeque. Eddie had carried the bike about ten feet away from the back porch into the backyard. Apparently, Eddie thought he could see better in the moonlight, without the roof above the porch casting its shadow onto him. Great. Now Eddie was fifteen feet away from us, and the bike was between him and us. There was no way we would be able to cover that distance without him seeing us coming. We needed a distraction. I was trying to think, but the thought that Eddie would be finished with breaking the bike any second was consuming my mind. No ideas were coming. Maybe we could wait for him to finish and then hope he put the broken bike back where he had found it, so we could pounce on him then.

Suddenly, a flash of light hit the windows behind AJ. It was Scooter! He had blinked the flashlight on for just a half-second and then shut it back off. It distracted Eddie enough that he dropped his backpack and stood up to face the woods. This was our one chance! I stood up and stepped off the porch. It took AJ a moment to realize what I was doing, so I stood exposed out in the open for what felt like eternity. Finally, AJ also stepped off the porch. As we moved forward, time seemed to stand still.

Crossing the twelve remaining feet to Eddie felt like running through water. I took a step. He must have heard me; he began to turn his head toward us. Scooter could see that Eddie was going to turn around, so he flashed the light again. Eddie, distracted again, focused his attention on the woods. I was almost there now. As we moved forward, AJ moved away from me, so the hammock stretched between us. One more step! The soft ground seemed to swallow my feet as I tried to keep running. I felt myself falling! I threw my side of the hammock up and over the bike, toward Eddie's back. AJ stayed on his feet, ran around the bike, and got his end of the hammock above Eddie's head.

Eddie let out a surprised yelp. He stumbled forward from the weight of the hammock. Preoccupied by watching the scene, I forgot to brace my fall. I let out a yelp of my own and face-planted into the dirt. Dirt stung my eyes and partially blinded me. Eddie tried to spin around to see what was attacking him. I heard him grunt as he twisted and became more entangled. AJ lunged to tackle Eddie. They both crashed on top of me. The high-schooler, Eddie, wasn't much bigger than AJ, but he had the fury of a cornered animal. Eddie flailed and kicked and yelled. As he and AJ wrestled, they both got tangled in the hammock together. With stinging eyes and a mouthful of dirt, I clambered to my knees but couldn't see much. Suddenly, I got a hard kick in the ribs, and I went flying into the bicycle. As I tried to untangle myself, I heard a loud *shhh* sound. *Did I pop a hole in the tire?* I dismissed the thought, turned around, and blindly threw myself on the pile that was Eddie and AJ. Light flashed in my face. Scooter must have been running over to help.

I took someone's elbow to my left ear. My ear instantly began pulsating in pain and ringing like crazy. I rolled off the dogpile in agony. With my other ear, I could now hear the desperate tweet of a whistle. *A little late, Traverna Lynn*, I thought. As I laid there, drops of water began to hit my face. *It can't be raining, can it?* I rolled over onto all fours, hoping to get my composure. That's when I realized that the sprinklers had come on. The dirt underneath me was already becoming wet enough to cake my clothes.

My eyes began to clear slightly, and I could see that Eddie had his feet free of the hammock. He was starting to stand up! AJ looked disoriented from getting a sprinkler sprayed right in his face. Scooter held onto the hammock for dear life, but he was no match for Eddie. Eddie managed to stand up. Scooter's flashlight laid on the moist ground. A beam of light shone from it right at Eddie's knees. He struggled to free his arms.

I had to act fast. I felt like that light was showing me the way. I lunged forward with all my might and hit Eddie squarely in the side of the knee. He screamed, and his legs gave out from underneath him. Eddie, Scooter, and I crashed into a pile on the ground. Scooter was now tangled in the hammock with Eddie. I felt a sharp pain in my side. I'd landed on a stick or something. *Am I injured? How bad is it? Am I going to die?* I yelled in a panic, "Get off! Get off!"

AJ half-wrestled, half-tackled the screaming Eddie to pull him off me. I rolled over to see what had caused my inevitable death. Water began gushing everywhere. I had landed on a sprinkler head, and it had broken off! So now water was spraying out of the ground like the fountains down at the waterfront park. In seconds, the dirt around me became a muddy mess.

Eddie no longer seemed interested in escaping. He began swinging his arms around in an effort to inflict pain equal to that in his left knee. We now tried to escape, but the ground was so slick that even crawling away was nearly impossible. With escape impossible, I tried to just stay low and avoid Eddie's flailing arms.

Just then, a hand grabbed my shoulder and pulled me backward, out of the fray. The grip seemed way too strong to be Eddie. I sat on my butt, blinking quickly and trying to wipe the mud out of my eyes in order to see what had just happened. As I tried to stand, the strong hand kept pressure on my shoulder, so I stayed seated. A sprinkler was spraying next to me, so I turned my face toward it and took a long spray in the face to wash the mud out of my eyes. I then turned and looked behind me to see a man in shorts, T-shirt, and bare feet staring back at me. He was not smiling.

I looked around and saw that several other men had a hold of Scooter, AJ, and Eddie. In the moonlight, I could see a few women talking over by the fence, an elderly man standing near them, and Traverna Lynn. Most everyone was dressed in pajamas. (Not Traverna Lynn, of course.) I guessed our little wrestling match had awakened most of the neighbors.

None of the men holding us were talking, so I decided that was probably a good idea and silently sat there. It didn't take long for a police officer to show up through the gate on the side of the house. The officer asked all the spectators to quickly file out of the backyard and give a statement to the officers who were waiting in the front of the house. He then went over to the man holding Eddie and said something too quiet for me to hear. The man handed Eddie to the officer and then motioned for the men holding AJ, Scooter, and me to come with him. As they left the backyard, a couple more police officers filed in and told the three of us to come with them. The first officer started putting Eddie in handcuffs.

When we walked out to the front of the house, we could see Eddie's car in the driveway. Apparently, he had figured he would just park in front of the house and try to act like it was his to begin to with. Unfortunately for him, as we later found out, the homeowners had asked the next-door neighbors to "keep an eye on the house" while they were on vacation. So as soon as Eddie had pulled into the driveway and walked around to the back of the house, the neighbors had called the police. When they had heard all the screaming coming from the backyard, they had decided they might need to do something themselves until the police responded to the call.

An officer made us sit on the curb next to the driveway and told us not to move unless we wanted to experience some handcuffs like Eddie. Out of fear and exhaustion, we did not move an inch. We watched as Eddie was escorted by an officer to a police car across the street. He was placed in the backseat, and the car quickly drove away.

Traverna Lynn sat down on the curb next to me. I'm not sure if she was told to or if she felt obligated to.

"Nice whistle," I whispered to her sarcastically, without even turning my head to look at her.

"Well, when I heard you guys yelling back there, I had no clue what was going on, but I figured drawing attention to you would either scare Eddie away or bring the neighbors to rescue you."

"Well, I guess it sort of worked," I mumbled as I rubbed my sore side. I wasn't really in the mood to be giving out compliments or thank-yous.

So there we sat, sopping wet, covered in mud, feeling like we had been run over by a train, waiting, and dreading to hear our fate.

CHAPTER 24
Competitive Detective

After fifteen painfully long minutes, another police car showed up. The driver drove past us, made a U-turn, and parked the car in the back of a long line of other police cars already at the scene. The driver turned off the engine but remained in the car for several more minutes. The driver's door finally opened, and before he even got out of the car, I knew it was Commander Coleman. I don't know how, but I just knew. He walked over and just stood there, looking down at us. He pursed his lips and shook his head in disbelief. After studying the three of us muddy boys he spoke.

"How did I know I would find the three of you here?" He let out a chuckle, "At least you were gentlemen and didn't let your lady friend get dirty too." He nodded at Traverna Lynn.

Just then another officer walked up holding Eddie's backpack. It was originally black, but it was so covered in mud that you'd think its natural color was brown. The officer handed Commander Coleman a pair of vinyl gloves, which the commander put on, and then handed him the dirty backpack. It was already partially unzipped, and we all held our breath as the commander pulled it open further and peered inside. We really hoped there would be some evidence inside so the police could connect it to some of the previous vandalisms; otherwise, our story about a series of crimes would be just that— a story. Commander Coleman rooted around in the bag for a couple seconds. He held the bag above our heads as he rummaged through it. This meant we couldn't see what he was seeing; we could just hear things clanking together inside. The combined feelings of anticipation and uncertainty over what he might find were absolute torture.

Eventually, Coleman let out a loud "Hmm" and pulled a piece of paper out of the bag. It was the list! I tried to hide the fact that I recognized it, but the best I could do was smile and give a "Who, me?" sort of look.

Commander Coleman quietly looked over the list, which was partially covered in mud, and then looked up to look at the four of us sitting on the curb. I don't know what the others were doing, but I was concentrating on not letting my face give away anything. Coleman stared at us for an uncomfortably long time and then broke into the biggest smile I'd ever seen on him, and then he began to laugh.

"Alright, you four. Get in the car; we're headed to

the station." He held out his hand to help Traverna Lynn up. Those of us who were muddy, battered, and bruised were left to get up on our own. I turned to look at Scooter and AJ. A quick shoulder shrug from Scooter and the puzzled looks on their faces told me that they were just as confused by Coleman's reaction as I was. We all walked silently to the commander's car and the three of us boys muddied up the back seat, while Traverna Lynn got to sit in the front.

In silence, the commander started the car and put it in drive. None of us dared talk on the drive to the police station. It was only ten minutes, but that was plenty of time for my mind to race for answers to what had just happened.

Why had the commander not asked us the question I had been dreading to answer? Why did he not ask how we knew Eddie would be there? It was almost like he already knew the answer. Did he know about us finding the list? How could he have known? He had seemed to change his attitude the moment he saw the list in Eddie's backpack. I thought we knew stuff the police didn't, but Commander Coleman was acting as if he knew more than we did. I hoped once we got to the station, the police would start providing answers and not ask us to provide any.

When we got to the police station, Commander Coleman took us straight to his office and told us to take seat. After taking a good look at us muddy boys in the brightness of the office overhead lights, he changed his mind and had us stay standing until an officer had brought in some towels from the locker rooms. Coleman watched as the chairs across from his desk were covered with towels by the officer. Only then were we allowed to sit down next to Traverna Lynn, who had long since taken her seat.

The commander turned to Traverna Lynn. "What is your phone number, young lady? I have to call your parents."

She gave him the number, and he wrote it down on a pad of paper from his desk. He then stood up and headed for the door. AJ tried to speak, but Coleman stopped him and pointed at the three of us. "I already have all of your phone numbers." With that, he smiled and walked out of the room.

The walls of Commander Coleman's office were made almost completely of glass, which allowed us to see nearly everything going on in the entire police station. I could see Eddie—still handcuffed—sitting in a chair next to a desk. He was talking very animatedly to the officer at the desk, who was asking questions and taking notes. I tried to read Eddie's lips, but I had very little success.

About ten minutes later, when Commander Coleman came back into his office, Traverna Lynn's dad, Mr. McIntyre, was with him. He did not look happy. In fact, I recognized that look; I had seen it before, when we saw him with Arwen at Fat Smitty's. (Man, that seems like a long time ago, doesn't it?)

Now that I think about it, I have only seen Mr. McIntyre two times, and both times he looked pretty ticked off. I hope that's not how he is all the time!

Anyway, Traverna Lynn and her dad quickly left, and then Coleman sat down at his desk, leaned forward, and stared at us with squinted eyes. "Well, I was wondering how you three seemed to always know where the crime was, even before we did," he began.

Uh-oh, here it comes, I thought. *He knows how we came across the list...*

He leaned back in his chair and laughed. "Ha! Well, I guess I should still give you some credit—I mean, you did try to give us help early on. We just didn't put the clues together very well. I am still a little curious how you knew, but I'm not sure I want to know."

I was a little confused as to what he meant by "give us help early on." What was he talking about? Did he mean the first time we'd come to ask about bike crimes?

He opened his desk drawer and pulled out a piece of paper. He looked down at the paper and then asked, "I am curious, though, what does 'A.F.' stand for?"

We couldn't help but look at each other now. Scooter had genuine shock on his face. AJ's jaw had dropped, and his eyes had opened wide. *So much for guarding our expressions!* But how could Commander Coleman know about A.F.? We hadn't told anyone about the coded message we'd found inside Scooter's book.

After all of us sputtering for a couple seconds, Scooter finally spoke intelligibly. "We have no clue what A.F. stands for."

Coleman continued to be amused. "Hey, if you don't want to tell me, that's okay. But if you want credit for solving the case, maybe you shouldn't be so mysterious."

"Sir?" Scooter asked in confusion.

The commander looked back at the paper on his desk. "'Stop him before it's too late'? C'mon, you can give a better clue than that!" he said as he held out the piece of paper to Scooter. Scooter leaned forward, grabbed the paper, and then sat back so AJ and I could read it with him. On the top of the paper, it said, "You'd better stop him before it's too late. —A.F." Then below that was a list of about ten addresses. I couldn't be sure, but I think those ten addresses were basically the last ten from Eddie's list. Some thought was starting to form in the back of my brain, but I couldn't quite form it into shape yet.

Scooter spoke up, holding the piece of paper up in the air. "Where did you get this?"

Commander Coleman laughed again and rolled his eyes. "It came *anonymously* in the mail a couple of days ago, but you already knew that. Honestly, I was a little slow putting it all together. I didn't really know what to do with that paper until I saw the similar list in Eddie's backpack. Then—or should I say, now, everything makes sense." He smiled in satisfaction. That nagging thought rolling around the back of my brain now came into clear focus, front and center: *Coleman thinks we sent him that list!*

Scooter began to stutter, "I don't... I... well... I—"

He was saved by a knock on the door frame of Commander Coleman's office. It was the officer who had been listening to Eddie.

"Did you get a confession?" Commander Coleman asked.

"Yes, sir, and much more."

"Really?" the commander said, intrigued, "Like what?"

The officer looked at us and then began walking over, presumably to whisper in the commander's ear so that we wouldn't be able to hear. The commander stopped him. "Oh, just share with the whole class. I mean, these boys probably know more than we do, anyway." He gave us a smile.

"Um, okay," the officer began. "Well, his story goes all the way back to the spray-painting of the junior high that we investigated at the end of this past school year. Eddie admits that he was the one who did that. But here's the thing: remember how during our investigation, we found that the security tape was missing from the junior high, and we wondered if there was even a tape to begin with? Apparently, there *was* a tape, and it showed up in a package on Eddie's doorstep the next day. With the tape was a note saying if he didn't do exactly what he was told, a copy of that tape would be sent to the police. He was supposed to go down a list of addresses, breaking a bicycle at each. The note included the list of addresses that we found in his backpack. Eddie felt like he had no choice, so he just started working his way down the list—"

The commander interrupted: "Wait, so why would someone give him a list of bicycles to break?"

"I don't know," the officer replied. "Maybe the person who sent the list thought Eddie would be more inclined to break bicycles than anything else. After all, he works at a bike shop. Anyway, the plan worked, and Eddie decided that this could actually work out well for him. He thought if he brought in more business, his boss would be happier and not get on his case as much."

"So that's it? What info do we have about the guy who sent Eddie the list of addresses?" Commander Coleman asked.

"Nothing. Apparently the video just showed up on Eddie's doorstep one day."

"Well, it sounds like we caught a small fish in Eddie, but there's an even bigger fish to catch now. We need to figure out who our mysterious friend is. Get over to Eddie's house and collect the videotape and any packaging it came in. And let's get that list of addresses that Eddie had with him and take it over to the lab to get analyzed. Maybe there is some evidence we can use there.

"During the spray-painting investigation, we had compiled a list of everyone who had worked at that junior high in the last two years. Let's dig that back up and look at it with fresh eyes. Whoever stole that videotape from the junior high probably had access because they worked there or knew someone who worked there."

"Yes, sir." The officer had his orders, and so he left.

Commander Coleman turned his attention back to the three of us. "Anything you boys would like to add? Any evidence you think they should be looking for when they head over to Eddie's house?"

We were all scared that if we said anything, we might slip up and say something that would give away our secret. So the three of us just gave blank stares in response. An uncomfortable silence followed, along with an awkward staring contest. Coleman was staring at us, and we were trying to look anywhere but at him.

Finally, he got out of his chair, walked around his desk and stood above us. "You guys need to be more careful. And I'm sure I don't need to remind you that breaking the law in order to enforce the law is still breaking the law. You guys know that, don't you?" He asked with a smile.

Not sure what to say, we all gave a hesitant, "Yes, sir." *He knows*, I thought to myself.

"Never forget that." He said as he walked toward the door. "Your parents will be here shortly." And then he was out the door.

As soon as Coleman was out of earshot, we all started talking at once. AJ was the first to be heard: "He knows about the house!"

"No, he doesn't," Scooter said, trying to calm him down.

"Then why did he just say that stuff about breaking the law to enforce the law?" I jumped in.

"I don't know! Maybe he was referring to our trespassing tonight? But whether he knows or not, it doesn't matter, anyway. If we were going to get in trouble for that, it would have already happened. I am more interested in who sent the police this note." He held up the piece of paper that Coleman had handed him.

"Coleman thinks it was us!" AJ said excitedly.

"Well, obviously, we didn't send it," Scooter answered. "But I don't think it hurts for the time being to let him continue to think we did."

"So Coleman thinks that A.F. is our 'other identity' that is helping the police solve crimes," I said. "But what about you, Scoot? Who do you think A.F. is?"

"And do you think that this A.F.—" AJ pointed at the paper in Scooter's hand, "—is the same A.F. who sent you the Sherlock Holmes book?"

"Of course it is," Scooter replied. "I think perhaps A.F. is our new competition or something. If we could pretty much solve this case on our own, then perhaps A.F. figured it out, too. If Arwen hired us, then maybe someone else on the address list hired A.F. My guess is, the message from A.F. in the book I have at home was more of a competitive taunt than the threat we originally perceived it to be."

"Sort of like an 'I bet I solve this case before you do' message?" I asked.

"Exactly," Scooter replied with a smile as he poked me lightly on the chest.

Just then Commander Coleman walked back into the room along with Mr. Seeva, Mr. Parks, and my mom. Of course, none of them were smiling now.

The commander spoke first. "Well, boys, we just talked to the owners of the house with the backyard that you made a mess of. They're going to have to come home earlier than they had planned, so naturally they are not very happy about it." He paused for dramatic effect.

"But after explaining the whole situation to them, they have agreed not to press charges against the three of you. In return, you agree to help them replant the backyard, which you helped to destroy. In addition, you will work some extra hours to pay for the sprinkler heads that they now need to replace. Agreed?"

"They agree," my mom said before we even had a chance to respond. "A little community service will be just the start of this boy's punishment." With that, she grabbed my ear and pulled me up out of my chair and right out the door. The last thing I saw was AJ and Scooter trying hard not to laugh as they watched me get pulled away. But I knew their sense of humor would not last long. Their fate was sealed, just like mine.

Epilogue

So as you can probably guess, I have been grounded to my room once again. Two weeks this time: for running around in the dark when I know I should be in bed, for lying to my mother and making her think I was at AJ's house when I wasn't, and for freaking my mom out in general. During our first major case, I was grounded for three weeks, but let me tell you, two weeks of summer stuck in the house is way worse than three weeks during the school year. At least I got to see my friends at school during that prison sentence.

So of course, I have been spending this time documenting our second major case, *The Case of the Bike in the Birdcage*. So by now you're pretty much caught up to the end of the story.

Except that there's this one really important part that you gotta know about because it is really rocking my world right about now!

As you might have concluded by now, I'm trying to be a little more thorough in my documentation this time around, so I have included extra information in this file. First, I logged all of the messages we received from The Network. I also printed off Eddie's list of addresses that Scooter emailed to me and the map showing where they all were. What else did I put in the file? Oh yeah, we got written up again in the newspaper, so I cut out the article and put that inside. That should drum up some business for us. We might need some free advertising, if there is a competitor out there now.

When I had done that, I still needed to mark all The Network-reported crimes on the same map as the actual addresses from Eddie's list, just to see how well The Network did at finding and reporting what the Enigma Squad asked them to. But I figured I wasn't in a hurry because I still had a few more days of Bedroom Confinement. Otherwise, I was almost done with the case file when the biggest thing happened. I was sitting on my bed, staring at the map of all of the addresses on Eddie's list, when I heard a knock on my bedroom door.

"Come in," I said, thinking it was either my sister or mother. I was mistaken; as the door opened, there stood a smiling Traverna Lynn.

"Hey," she said shyly, "Your mom said you were grounded to your room but she said I could say a quick hello."

"Uh, hello," I said, obviously surprised. "What are you doing here?"

"I came by because I wanted to thank you. If you

remember, I was trying to figure out who spray-painted the junior high at the end of the school year, and apparently Eddie confessed to doing that. He never would have been caught if it weren't for you guys."

"Hey, you obviously helped," I added.

"Yeah, well, I'm still thankful. You know what they say, 'Never kiss a gift horse in the mouth.'"

"Uh, no. Nobody says that," I said, shaking my head.

"Whatever," she said dismissively. "I also came by to give you your payment." She stepped toward the bed and handed me a handful of bills.

"What?" I asked, confused.

"Arwen did say she would pay you, didn't she?" Traverna Lynn asked. "So here you go."

I instinctively started counting the money. Two hundred dollars! I looked up at her, and only then did I realize that what I had just done was probably rude. "Oh, uh, sorry. I just wasn't expecting anything at all, let alone this much!"

"Well, you did solve the case. And besides, between you and me, most of this money didn't come from Arwen, anyway. It came from my dad."

"Really?"

"Yeah, he was pretty ticked at first. But once I told him the whole story about how we worked together, he insisted that you get paid, since you were hired to do a job and you got the job done."

"Wow, I never would have thought... So what did

Arwen have to say about the case?"

"Not much. I think she was just happy to get back on dad's good side—that's all she really cared about anyway."

"Yeah, I am starting to get that impression," I said, defeated. "Well… thank you… and him… and I guess Arwen."

"You're welcome," she said as she looked at the file in my lap. "So what are you doing now?"

"Oh, just sort of wondering about these addresses," I said, holding the map out for her to see. "Why were these addresses the ones picked for the list? Is it because they all had accessible bicycles to break? Or did they have some other thing in common? There seems to be no connection between the houses at all."

"Well, there is the A.F. connection," she laughed, turning and walking toward the door.

"Yeah," I said, laughing right along with her. *Oh, wait!* My mind began racing to put together a timeline. *Traverna Lynn didn't know about the book, and she had left the police station before Commander Coleman showed us the list. So how could she know about A.F.?*

"Uh, wait, Traverna Lynn, what are you talking about?"

"The purple line, silly!" she answered with another laugh. "I'm joking of course, but you do have that purple line that runs through all your addresses. So there is at least *something* connecting them. Hey, I gotta run. We'll talk soon, maybe when you get done being grounded." She laughed again as she headed down the hallway and then down the stairs.

I sat for a moment, confused. I looked back down at the map in front of me. I could now see what Traverna Lynn was talking about. There was a faint purple line that connected all the address dots together. The line had been drawn by the map program Scooter had used to plot the addresses. As I stared at that purple line, the hair on the back of my neck slowly began to rise. It all made sense now. "Order must be maintained!" Only now could I see what Traverna Lynn had seen instantly, something I could have seen if I had just connected the dots in order. Something had been there the whole time, but the Enigma Squad had overlooked it. There on the map in front of me—taunting me—was the purple line connecting all the dots to spell out those two now-familiar capital letters.